## THE LUNATIC REPUBLIC

In 1997 under the auspices of the Celestial Chinese Republic a rocket containing Tin Pan, a Chinese scientist, and John Bosworth, an English commercial traveller, went up from the Gobi desert to reach the Moon. They discovered that the barren wilderness on the side of the Moon visible to the Earth was not caused by volcanic action or meteorite bombardment, but by a nuclear war 3,000 years ago between two peoples each determined to preserve its own way of life. From this disastrous conflict a comparatively small tract on the other side of the Moon managed to survive and, as the Lunatic Republic, to carry to its technological conclusion the way of life toward which humanity already seems tending.

# BY COMPTON MACKENZIE

## Novels and Romances

SINISTER STREET
SYLVIA SCARLETT
GUY AND PAULINE
CARNIVAL
FIGURE OF EIGHT
CORAL
THE VANITY GIRL
ROGUES AND VAGABONDS
THE ALTAR STEPS
THE PARSON'S PROGRESS
THE HEAVENLY LADDER
HUNTING THE FAIRIES
WHISKY GALORE
ROCKETS GALORE
KEEP THE HOME GUARD
    TURNING
THE MONARCH OF THE GLEN
THE RIVAL MONSTER
THE RED TAPEWORM
POOR RELATIONS
APRIL FOOLS
RICH RELATIVES
BUTTERCUPS AND DAISIES
WATER ON THE BRAIN
VESTAL FIRE
EXTRAORDINARY WOMEN
THIN ICE
EXTREMES MEET
THE THREE COURIERS
OUR STREET
THE DARKENING GREEN
THE PASSIONATE ELOPEMENT
FAIRY GOLD
THE SEVEN AGES OF WOMAN
THE OLD MEN OF THE SEA
THE FOUR WINDS OF LOVE:
    THE EAST WIND
    THE SOUTH WIND
    THE WEST WIND
    THE NORTH WIND

## Play

THE LOST CAUSE

## Verse

POEMS 1907
KENSINGTON RHYMES

## History and Biography

EASTERN EPIC. VOL I
ALL OVER THE PLACE
GALLIPOLI MEMORIES
ATHENIAN MEMORIES
GREEK MEMORIES
AEGEAN MEMORIES
WIND OF FREEDOM
MR ROOSEVELT
DR BENEŠ
PRINCE CHARLIE
PRINCE CHARLIE AND HIS
    LADIES
CATHOLICISM AND SCOTLAND
MARATHON AND SALAMIS
PERICLES
THE WINDSOR TAPESTRY
THE VITAL FLAME
I TOOK A JOURNEY
COALPORT
THE SAVOY OF LONDON
REALMS OF SILVER
THE QUEEN'S HOUSE
SUBLIME TOBACCO

## Essays and Criticism

ECHOES
A MUSICAL CHAIR
UNCONSIDERED TRIFLES
REAPED AND BOUND
LITERATURE IN MY TIME

## Children's Stories

SANTA CLAUS IN SUMMER
TOLD
MABEL IN QUEER STREET
THE UNPLEASANT VISITORS
THE CONCEITED DOLL
THE ENCHANTED BLANKET
THE DINING-ROOM BATTLE
THE ADVENTURES OF TWO
    CHAIRS
THE ENCHANTED ISLAND
THE NAUGHTYMOBILE
THE FAIRY IN THE WINDOW BOX
THE STAIRS THAT KEPT ON
    GOING DOWN

# THE LUNATIC REPUBLIC

*By*

Compton Mackenzie

1959

CHATTO & WINDUS

LONDON

PUBLISHED BY
Chatto and Windus Ltd
LONDON

\*

Clarke, Irwin & Co. Ltd
TORONTO

PRINTED IN GREAT BRITAIN BY
T. & A. CONSTABLE LTD.

To
Wilfred and Jane
Macartney
affectionately

# CONTENTS

## Chapter 1

I RICHARD BOSWORTH was ten years old when the U.S.S.R. launched their first sputniks, and I remember my father, who was very proud of having been born a day before Queen Victoria died, saying that people who could shoot off an innocent dog to die up in the air ought to be exterminated. I remember gazing at one of the small black-and-white television sets we had in those days and thinking that the 'bleep' coming out of a lot of squiggles on the screen was the whining of poor Little Lemon, the dog, as it went whirling round above the Earth.

Two years later my poor father died of blood poisoning after being bitten by an Alsatian, and I remember my mother saying to my grandmother that if John (John Bosworth was my father's name) had cared a little more for people and a little less for dogs he might still be alive. I was shocked to hear her say this because I was just as fond of dogs as my father and attached great importance to the little metal bone I wore in my buttonhole to show I was a Woofer, that is a member of the Woofers and Waggers League.

I wonder if my mother watched the launching of Heavenly Dragon; that was the name the Chinese gave to the rocket in which Tin Pan and I were shot off to the Moon from the Gobi Desert on 21st June 1997. I did give her a splendid television set before I left for China, soon after she had gone to live in N.W. 107. She had always wanted to live in Oxford for sentimental reasons because she and my father had spent their honeymoon touring in a funny old car called a Morris Minor, which was made in Oxford by the man whose

A *

munificence enabled a decaying university of the old type to modernise itself and become the leading technological university in the world. So when the city of Oxford was taken over by the London County Council my mother managed to find a flat on the fifteenth storey of one of the new Council towers in Cowley.

Although so many rockets were successfully sent to the Moon during the 'sixties and 'seventies, the prospect of landing human beings there remained dim. It was not until after the Three Days War of 1987 with the U.S.S.R. that the victorious Prosperity Union of Asia was able to devote all its attention to conquering space. The Chinese, as the predominant influence in the Union of Asia, revived the old notion of a Celestial Empire, and the Celestial Chinese Republic was determined to annex the Moon in due course and to incorporate it in the Prosperity Union of Asia as a satellite country. They must be feeling very pleased with themselves, for although as yet they have not succeeded in landing any more people on the Moon since Tin Pan and I arrived here over a year ago, I have no doubt they will, and I expect the next party will be equipped with more reliable means of communication with the Earth than Tin Pan and I were given. It is strange to reflect now that when I was a young man we were still obsessed by the fear of Russian domination. If I ever have any readers, they may be wondering why I, as a citizen of the Welfare State of Europe, should have been shot off to the Moon in a Chinese rocket. The answer is that I was sent there because the Chinese wanted to have a European witness to testify to the truth of their claim to have reached the Moon. The Russians after their defeat indulged in the same kind of propaganda about the Chinese as the Americans used to indulge in about them once upon a time, and it is easy to understand why they should have taken pleasure in denigrating every new invention the Chinese produced. One might have thought, after the Chinese had made oil valueless by their discovery of venusium in that part of Antarctica which was ceded to them by the Russians at the Peace of Peking (and thus by gaining a monopoly of cheap nuclear power made the rest of the world dependent upon them) that the Russians would have acknowledged their technological supremacy. No amount of propaganda was of any avail against the prospect of turning the arid deserts of Arabia and even the vast expanse of central Australia into the most fertile land on earth within another twenty years. Nevertheless, the Russians seemed unable to shake off the belief that they were still the scientific leaders of the world, and so the childish propaganda continued.

I went to China in 1996 to negotiate for a supply of venusium which my firm in England wanted to import in the hope of selling it to the Israeli administration of Egypt. At that date the Chinese were getting rather worried about the growing influence of Israel in world affairs. When Egypt was decontinentalised in 1985 and declared to be neither Asian, African nor European, the Israelis seemed to be the obvious people to administer it, and the success they made of the job led to a good deal of Chinese apprehensiveness about the future of Africa. So in 1995 they put an embargo upon the supply of venusium to the Israeli Administration. The fact was that the Chinese, whose success in discovering how to make gold had compelled the Americans to withdraw from any further attempts to dominate the Eurasian continent and to concentrate upon making America, from Alaska to Patagonia, an economic entity through social credit, were determined to prevent if possible any comparable financial upset in the Eastern Hemisphere.

They did not want the Israelis, in developing Africa, to discover an element comparable with venusium. Their attitude was a relic of the bad old policy of obstructing the development of other nations which, faithfully pursued for so long, had almost led the world to irrevocable ruin. I have no doubt that by now the Chinese have realised their mistake, and I pray that human beings will soon collaborate to exploit space and that the record I am now making of what it is like on the other side of the moon may be taken back by myself to Boojumania. Yes, that is the name they give to our Earth in the Lunatic Republic. Nevertheless, even if a party of Boojums should arrive, I do not feel perfectly confident that the Lunatics will allow me or any other Boojums who get here to go back to where they came from. However, that is for the future to decide.

When I reached China in 1996 I was received with the greatest friendliness and the negotiations were proceeding in a most satisfactory way until an unfortunate accident occurred. While I was packing for the flight from London to Peking I had slipped into my pocket a tattered old copy of a book published nearly fifty years ago called *Nineteen-Eighty-Four*. Why I bothered to take a book for a journey of an hour or two I don't know, but after all the only chance we ever get nowadays of reading for amusement is when we are travelling, and I am still sufficiently old-fashioned to enjoy dipping into an uninstructive book occasionally, for I used to be a great reader when I was a small boy. I left this old book lying about in the room at my hotel, and about a week after I arrived it vanished. I paid no attention to this at the time because I knew how much the Chinese disliked being reminded of their agelong static past by the sight of anything that seemed at all old, and I supposed that one of the hotel staff had thrown it away in disgust.

However, what had happened was that the book had been handed over to the secret police, who had detected in it an attempt to subvert the position of President Ba Li-hu.

That evening I was arrested and questioned. I tried to explain that this was an old-fashioned novel published nearly fifty years ago which had attempted to draw a fanciful picture of what the world might be like in 1984 and that Big Brother had nothing whatever to do with Ba Li-hu. It was no use; my explanation was disregarded and I was put in prison, where I remained for over six months in solitary confinement fed entirely upon millet. Then abruptly my dietary was changed and I was regaled with all the resources of Chinese cooking, on which in spite of the loneliness I throve physically. I was not allowed to read even the technological books used in the education of Chinese youth, but, to impress me with the progress of the Union of Asia, television was switched on at intervals throughout the afternoon and evening. The smallness of my cell made watching the television, which took up almost the whole of one wall, an almost intolerable strain upon the eyes. Moreover, as most of the viewing offered nothing but Chinese teenagers, male and female, doing gymnastic exercises and performing mass movements in patterns, the strain upon the mind was not less intense. The only variety consisted of similar displays by Indonesian, Japanese, Burmese, Tibetan, Indian and Cinghalese youth: it was like watching a well-drilled ant-heap.

At last one morning two Chinese officers arrived in my cell and ordered me to follow them. I found I was to be the subject of what seemed an endless medical examination. I believe I can say that the only part of me they omitted to examine with tedious thoroughness was a mole on my left cheek; a mole on my left shoulder had occupied the doctors for an hour. At the end of five days, when I was taken back to my cell, I was told that there would be something of great interest on television next day.

"Not another youth congress?" I moaned.

"No, I am afraid it will not be a youth congress," said one of the officers, speaking to my great surprise in excellent English, for I had never suspected during his visits of inspection throughout the last nine months that he spoke a word of it. "You will not see again youth gatherings, at any rate on Earth."

"Thank God for that," I muttered.

He looked at me with a smile of what I could not be sure was compassion or contempt.

"On Earth," he repeated gently.

"Where else would I see them?"

"If all goes well, as we hope that it will, you may perhaps see a youth congress on the Moon."

I laughed politely to show that I appreciated his humour.

"No, no, I am not as you say trying to be funny. You have successfully passed the very severe test of your physical condition and therefore you have been granted the privilege of being one of the first two human beings to descend on the Moon. The other is a Chinese gentleman, Mr Tin Pan. You are very fortunate, Mr Bosworth. If you had failed in the physical test, you would not be here at all now because you have made propaganda against Ba Li-hu."

I asked Sing Song if he seriously believed that the possession of a book fifty years old was deliberate propaganda. He made a deprecatory gesture.

"We do not believe anything for ourselves. We believe what we are told to believe by those who are wiser than we are," he replied gravely.

"Well, I think the sooner I get to the Moon the better," I exclaimed.

"It is a pleasure for us that it is a pleasure for you," Sing Song replied, and with a gentle inclination of the head he retired.

How little did I realise when I turned over to sleep that night, after a dinner even more delicious than usual that for the last three months I had been fattened up to sustain what I think without exaggeration I can call the greatest ordeal a human being could be compelled to undergo.

I was woken early next morning and taken to one of the airfields from which passenger traffic was excluded. A quarter of an hour after taking off, we landed in the midst of the most depressing landscape I had hitherto seen in all my life.

"We are now in the Gobi Desert," I was told by Sing Song, in whose charge I was. "It is hot in summer but in winter it is very cold, and there is much wind."

"There is plenty of wind now," I said, looking at the haze of dust which on every side bounded the waste of yellowish-grey clay across a cement track over which we walked a hundred yards to a large transparent building, inside which was gathered a large group of people.

"I must now ask you to cover your face, please," Sing Song said, handing me a plastic extinguisher with two slits for my eyes. "Television will begin when you arrive. This is a great moment for all the world. We announced last night that at noon precisely Heavenly Dragon would leave the Earth for the Moon with two human passengers. When the Americans were celebrating the five hundredth anniversary of the discovery of America, five years ago, they boasted they would land on the Moon within a year or two. I think, as you say, this will take the gold off the gingerbread for them."

"You're not seriously proposing to shoot me up to the Moon?" I gasped.

"But certainly we shall," Sing Song replied. "The only pity is that your name cannot be known to the world. You will never be what you call a Big Shot. I am afraid you will always be the Unknown Explorer. The fame of the discovery of the Moon must always belong to the greatest nation on Earth, and so Mr Tin Pan will have all the glory."

"If I'm to be unknown, I don't see the point of shooting me up to the Moon at all," I protested.

"Because you will tell the world before you are put in Heavenly Dragon that you have volunteered to go with Mr Tin Pan, as you say, for cricket."

"For cricket? What on earth—I mean what has cricket got to do with it?"

"Is not that what you call fair play? We wish the world to be sure that this is not a high story. . . . I beg pardon, tall story for glorification of China without truth."

"Then my name *will* be known."

"No."

"I shall tell the world."

"I do not think so," Sing Song murmured gently.

By this time we had reached the large transparent building, and I was immediately taken into one of the inner offices, where I was told to record the following announcement:

"I am an Englishman who for the last nine months has had the honour of being prepared for the greatest adventure any Englishman has undertaken. In a few minutes, accompanied by Mr Tin Pan, the distinguished Chinese scientist, I shall be on my way to the Moon. I regret that I cannot give you my name, but the Celestial Chinese Government speaking in the name of the mighty Prosperity Union of Asia has decided to make it clear to the future that the glory of reaching the Moon for the first time should belong exclusively to China. I am to enjoy a humble share of this glory only because the persistent attempts by the United American States, the Welfare State of Europe and the U.S.S.R. to foster disbelief in the scientific achievements of China has made it seem necessary to have an English witness to this supreme achievement. Mr Tin Pan and I are both confident that the world will hear of Heavenly Dragon's arrival on the Moon at noon to-morrow, 22nd June 1997. Whether Mr Tin Pan will be able to establish communication with the Earth remains to be seen."

"Wouldn't 'remains to be heard' be more accurate?" I suggested. The emendation was accepted.

"Should Mr Tin Pan be successful and should it be proved that Chinese scientific accomplishment has made it possible for human beings to exist on the Moon I shall have the honour of testifying that the enterprise was contrived and carried out entirely by Chinese imagination and technical skill. Finally, the Celestial Chinese Government authorises me to announce that if Mr Tin Pan and I succeed in landing on the Moon there is a possibility that it will appear blue when it rises to-morrow night, an explanation of which phenomenon will be given in due course."

"But what will be the use of my sending this rigmarole without telling people who I am?"

"You cannot tell people who you are because you have been dead now for nearly six months."

"What on earth are you talking about?"

"Yes, you are still on Earth for a few minutes longer," Sing Song murmured with a slow smile. "But seriously, Mr Bosworth, we have made enquiries and found that you are a bachelor without family, and that your mother, now over eighty, lives in London N.W. 107. Provision has been made for her through the Ambassador of the Celestial Chinese Republic in England. It was announced that you were regrettably killed in an airplane accident in the course of negotiations for the importation of venusium. Now will you please record what has been written for you?"

"But somebody is bound to recognise my voice."

"It is possible that someone will say 'that is the voice of Mr Bosworth'. But it will never be known for certain unless we are able to bring you back within a year, which is perhaps still a little doubtful. Now, will you please record what has been written."

I debated with myself for some moments whether I would obey Sing Song, but common sense, which has always been my ruling passion, warned me that if I refused I should either be put to death or at best pass the rest of my life in a Chinese prison. So I did what Sing Song had ordered me to do.

"And now," he said, giving me the extinguisher again, "I shall present you to Ba Li-hu. Please follow me."

My heart leapt. I should have an opportunity to make a last desperate appeal to the man who for as long as he should be able to sustain his position would be the embodiment of the Union of Asia, in all its apparently unassailable domination of the twenty-first century. When I saw him I saw that he was exactly like millions of other Chinese, which no doubt was one of the secrets of his influence. When he spoke, all China seemed to speak.

"You are a very lucky man, Mr Bosworth," Ba Li-hu observed when I had taken off the extinguisher which had concealed my features from the curious eyes watching my progress through the large transparent building to his heavily guarded and obfuscated sanctum.

"Lucky to have been chosen to accompany Mr Tin Pan on this historic date in the progress of the human race," he went on.

I suddenly felt convinced that nothing I could say would persuade Ba Li-hu to let me remain on Earth. A moment later he took up from the table in front of him a round silver disc attached to a silver ribbon.

"It is my pleasure, Mr Bosworth, to attach to your breast this medal. You are now a Hero of the Moon. I congratulate you on having won this very high honour. Mr Tin Pan has already been decorated and now awaits you to enter Heavenly Dragon."

I gave up the notion of appealing to Ba Li-hu to be left on Earth, and decided to accept the inevitable.

"I have one favour to ask of you, Comrade Ba Li-hu."

He frowned.

"It is that if you are satisfied that Mr Tin Pan and I have reached the Moon you will allow my name to be published. There will be some who may recognise my voice and it will be a great satisfaction to my friends to be able to tell all their friends that they knew the man who reached the Moon. It would also gratify my old mother."

"But we have already announced that you were killed in an air accident, Mr Bosworth."

"That is so, Comrade Ba Li-hu, but it could be announced that thanks to the miraculous skill of Chinese surgeons I recovered, and that owing to my desire . . . my desire, Comrade Ba Li-hu . . . to have the privilege of sharing in the great Chinese achievement, I had wished for security reasons to exist apparently no longer."

"I will make no promise, Mr Bosworth, but I will consider your request when we are sure that you have landed on the Moon. And now it is time for you to take your place in Heavenly Dragon."

Ba Li-hu offered me his hand.

"Yes, you are a very lucky man, Mr Bosworth," he declared once more.

I asked if I might put one more question to him.

"With pleasure."

"You didn't really believe, did you, that that old book by George Orwell was propaganda against you?"

He smiled grimly.

"I am not a stupid man, Mr Bosworth."

"I'm glad to hear you say that because it was worrying me to think that I was leaving so much of the Earth under the influence of a stupid man. May I ask the real reason for choosing me for this adventure?"

"Because we wanted an Englishman to go with Mr Tin Pan. Should the Moon be inhabited, which of course we consider highly improbable, we thought that the inhabitants were likely to learn Basic English more quickly than any other language, and as you know Basic English is now a compulsory subject in all Asia. Yes, it is so reassuring to know that wherever one finds oneself in the world one can always ask for hot water or the whereabouts of the W.C. Basic English has been your country's greatest achievement, Mr Bosworth, and since you partly simplified your spelling it is in my opinion firmly established as a world-wide method of communication. In addition to that, the reputation that the English still have for telling the truth—quite undeservedly let me add—suggested that an Englishman would be the most suitable companion for Mr Tin Pan. And now Heavenly Dragon is becoming impatient. Good-bye, Mr Bosworth, and a pleasant journey to the Moon."

Ba Li-hu shook my hand. Sing Song stepped forward

with the extinguisher for my face and then led the way
to what looked like a large black bee-hive inside which
Tin Pan and I were to be dressed in lunar equipment,
which I may observe bore very slight resemblance to
the space-suits delineated by the illustrators of boys'
books and the dramas of space-adventure shown on
television.

Tin Pan and I shook hands cordially before we were
dressed, after which as I saw him from within my headpiece he looked like a giant insect with six legs, the upper
two being his own arms and the other four supplemen-
tary arms which apparently he could use as easily as his
own, and with which he was presumably to work the
instruments of Heavenly Dragon. I suppose that I must
have looked like him, but without Tin Pan's extra arms.
We were both able to walk without too much difficulty,
and in spite of the weight to mount the steps leading up
to the entrance of the great ball in the middle of the
enormous rocket, which was at least a hundred feet high.

Thanks to television, millions of people saw what
Heavenly Dragon looked like on that morning of the
Twenty-First of June, 1997, and there is no need for me
to describe the outward appearance of that enormous
ball, fixed between two enormous tubes. Unfortunately,
at the time I was being educated, technology in some
form or another was not a compulsory subject at schools
and universities. Therefore I am unable to describe the
outside or the inside of Heavenly Dragon in technical
terms.

When I say that inside the ball I had the impression
that I was reclining in a comfortable chair amid a countless number of complicated instruments, that is all I can
say. When the entrance to the ball was closed, every
sound without was so muted that the explosion which
started the rocket moonwards sounded no more than

the noise of one of the old railway trains of my youth emerging from a tunnel. This was followed by a silence out of which came the level voice of Tin Pan.

"Can you hear me, Mr Bosworth?"

"Distinctly. Can you hear me, Mr Tin Pan?"

"Yes, I hear you distinctly, Mr Bosworth. Can you see the thin flexible tube leading from my mouth?"

"I can see a tube hanging from where your mouth would be if I could see your mouth."

"You have the same tube. When you feel hungry, push it through the aperture until you can put the end of it in your mouth. You will imbibe two drops of liquid with a pleasant taste and find it very strengthening both to your body and your mind. At our present rate of progress we should get to the end of our journey about twelve o'clock to-morrow morning and descend on the Moon as near as possible to the other side as we have been able to calculate. We shall be protected against the extreme heat by our equipment and equally against the extreme cold. Our nourishment will last for a year. . . ."

"A year?" I broke in.

"If we do not exceed six drops a day, and if the celestium proves efficacious."

"The celestium?"

"That is the name of the new secret effluence which it is estimated will supply atmosphere fit for human beings. And let me assure you, Mr Bosworth, we have every hope that it will prove efficacious."

"You sound very confident, Mr Tin Pan."

"I hope for much."

Whether it was the result of the speed at which we were travelling or whether it was merely emotional exhaustion I do not know, but almost immediately after Tin Pan's last remark I fell asleep. How long I slept I do not know either, but when I woke up and asked my companion what the time was he did not reply. In sudden terror of finding myself alone in Heavenly Dragon I shouted to Tin Pan. Suppose while I had been sleeping he had made that last and longest journey of all?

"Tin Pan! Tin Pan! Tin Pan, where are you?"

"I am here, Mr Bosworth," came the quiet voice of my companion.

"What is the time?"

"We have been travelling for about five hours. You can call it fifty thousand miles. Are you not feeling hungry?" he asked.

I decided that I was feeling hungry and told him so.

"Squeeze the tube twice and swallow two drops. Not more, please."

I did as he directed and received the impression that I had eaten half a dozen bananas and drunk a glass of milk.

"Your hunger is satisfied, no?" Tin Pan enquired.

"Yes, I feel perfectly satisfied."

"Mr Bosworth, if we should unfortunately come down in such a place as Ptolemy's Circus . . ."

"Ptolemy's Circus," I exclaimed. "Where on earth— I mean where in the moon—is that?"

"It is a name given by the old astronomers to one of these still mysterious flat expanses on the Moon. Some argue that they are the result of volcanic action. Others are of the opinion that they consist of great expanses of meteoric dust a mile or more deep, which might mean that we should be engulfed in it. I thought it was right for me to warn you."

"Thank you very much."

"Should that happen, I shall turn off the supply of celestium."

"And what would happen then?"

"You would immediately go to sleep and never wake up."

I suppose I ought to try to describe more accurately what my sensations were during this first flight to the Moon, but in fact I seemed to be without sensation and to be sitting there in a soundless vacuum. Anyway, if this account of mine is ever found by human beings who have flown to the Moon themselves, they will know what it felt like. I confess I should like posterity to commemorate me as well as Tin Pan, and if somebody from Earth is now reading what I am writing I do hope that he will have my account sent off by the first rocket launched from the Moon.

"We shall be down in about ten minutes now," the quiet voice of Tin Pan was saying as I emerged from about the twentieth nap of that journey. I imbibed two more drops of liquid, and apparently full of bananas and milk I composed myself to face eternity or extinction.

There was a bump followed by another lesser bump followed again by a final slight bump. Heavenly Dragon had arrived.

"Wait, while I release the celestium," Tin Pan told me.

Half an hour later Tin Pan pressed the button which opened the great ball in which we had been travelling and we could survey the lunar scene. Under a black sky sown with stars of almost dazzling brilliance stretched an endless waste of grey, pocked with the huge craters with which we have so long been familiar in photographs of the Moon. Tin Pan put a tube out of the mouth of the equipment in which he was enclosed.

"Cold but perfectly good air. The celestium has justified the enormous expense of making it."

He closed the opening of Heavenly Dragon.

"I must now signal our arrival to Earth."

He got out of his equipment and immediately to my dismay his face turned a vivid greenish-blue.

"Mr Tin Pan," I exclaimed, "your face and hands are blue."

"That is a minor inconvenience of the new effluence. We do not know yet whether the blue is permanent, but we hope that it may not be. There is no internal inconvenience. Do not be alarmed."

Tin Pan turned to one of the instruments which covered the inside of Heavenly Dragon and began to operate it. If his face had not been blue already, I am sure that the despair upon it would have made it seem blue.

"What's the matter?" I asked anxiously. "Are you in pain?"

"I am in the most intense pain of the mind that I have ever known. The radio is dead."

He pressed button after button in a series of agitated arpeggios, but there was no response.

"We have failed," he moaned.

"We've landed safely on the Moon. You can hardly call that failure," I protested.

"But what is the use of reaching the Moon if we cannot tell them anything about it on the Earth?"

"By the way, I didn't see the Earth in the sky just now," I said. "Perhaps that's why we can't get them."

"When the Moon is full to the Earth, there is no Earth to see. It is when the Moon is new that the Earth is full. But that would not affect radio communication. What can have gone wrong? It was the one thing that seemed perfectly safe. We were not sure that we should land successfully. We were not sure that the celestium would do what we hoped. But the radio was so certain."

"Don't atmospherics often interfere with it? Perhaps it doesn't like this new atmosphere you've provided."

"Mr Bosworth, you may be right," Tin Pan declared gravely. "We omitted to try the effect of celestium. I hope Dr Wang See-saw will not be disgraced."

"Who's he?"

"He is the scientist who discovered celestium. And he was looking forward so eagerly to being created a Hero of the Moon."

I wonder if I shall ever know if the full moon that rose for Earth that night was a blue moon.

We let some hours pass and then went out to look at the starlight in that black sky which was shedding a brightness beyond any that the Moon can shed on Earth, and when we woke next morning they were still shining in that black sky.

"The celestium has exceeded all our expectations," Tin Pan declared. "It has provided the Moon with atmosphere. I hope you will not be shocked when you look at yourself in the glass, Mr Bosworth."

Tin Pan's face was greenish-blue, but mine when I looked at it was a rich ultramarine. I suppose a Red-skin's would have been purple and a Negro's the colour of blue-black ink.

"We will wait for a day or two here," Tin Pan said. "And then if we find that the effect of the celestium persists it will be our duty to reach the other side of the Moon. If Heavenly Dragon landed according to our calculations, we should not be more than fifty miles or so away from it."

That fifty-mile struggle across what I thought then was either the horrible volcanic or meteorite dust cannot be described. Try to imagine what it was like in the equipment we were compelled to wear in order to survive a temperature which according to Tin Pan was over a hundred degrees below zero during this lunar sunlessness on this side lasting a fortnight. The only thing that sustained my spirit was the sight of the blue crescent Earth four times as large as the crescent Moon which every night grew larger until the earthlight made that ghastly lunar landscape as bright as the Earth's daylight.

"Do not despair, Mr Bosworth," Tin Pan said sedately, "in another two or three days I believe that we shall reach the other side of the Moon."

"It will probably be exactly the same as this side of the Moon except that we shall not see the Earth."

Three nights later the Earth failed to rise, and presently we found ourselves in a sort of twilight on a wide smooth road and saw on the horizon that the sky was lighted by the same kind of glow that one sees at night above great cities on Earth.

"The temperature is mild and pleasant," Tin Pan said. "You can take off your headpiece, Mr Bosworth."

I did so and saw that the greenish-blue of Tin Pan's face was now a clear Cambridge blue in the brilliant starlight.

"You are now a celestial blue, Mr Bosworth," he said. "Can it be that the atmosphere on the other side of the Moon is already subject to the influence of celestium?"

"Don't ask me," I said. "I'm an ignoramus about such matters."

## Chapter 2

THE relief of not having to drag our feet out of that infuriating dust, and of being able to take off my headpiece and to breathe as naturally as if we were back on Earth, gave me so much pleasure that I did not ask any questions about the future, and I was almost startled when Tin Pan said: "This road suggests that the other side of the Moon contradicts every scientific theory."

There was a note of anxious depression in his voice such as you might hear in the tone of a seminarist or a local preacher whose faith in the supernatural had been disturbed by some new scientific achievement. "Nothing that was revealed to us by the great new telescope we built in Tibet suggested any possibility of life existing on the Moon. We assumed, and we had every right to assume, that it would be exactly like the side visible from Earth." He shook his head. "Do you know, Mr Bosworth, I am almost glad that we did not establish communication with Earth, for if I had told them that we had detected signs of habitation on the other side of the Moon I might have been accused of inventing something for my own glorification and I might have been expelled from the Celestial Academy of Science."

It was my turn to shake my head.

"There's the difference between the Welfare State of Europe and the Prosperity Union of Asia. In England I should probably have received a fat television contract and been elected a Fellow of the Royal Society."

"But the Celestial Academy of Science would have been justified in expelling me."

"Why?"

"Because I might have been accused of trying to set

up my own opinion against the unanimous opinion of the Celestial Academy. And we have to admit, Mr Bosworth, that this road along which we are now walking is the only indication we yet have of lunar habitation."

Tin Pan had hardly made what he obviously intended to be a recantation of his presumptuous heresy to his fellow-members of the Celestial Academy of Science 240,000 miles away when we saw marching towards us along this surprising road a squad of men hardly four feet high with blue faces, all looking exactly alike and all dressed in blue breeches fitting close to the leg and blue shirts with wide collars open at the neck, on the front of which was woven or stamped a monosyllable with a number attached like those on the plates of motor-cars on Earth.

Some of my readers may have seen in childhood the original pictures of the mid-nineteenth century children's books *Alice in Wonderland* and *Alice Through the Looking Glass*. There have been a number of feeble attempts to re-illustrate the books since they went out of copyright and these are useless for comparison; but a reader who has seen those original drawings of Tweedledum and Tweedledee by Tenniel will have some idea of the expression on the blue faces of these lunar inhabitants. However, I must add that although their figures were paunchy like Tweedledum's and Tweedledee's, they all had exceptionally large domed heads and what I thought at first was a lamp on top but which on a closer view proved to be luminous hair. Every one of these creatures was exactly like his neightbour, and let me say here that, although I have now been living on the Moon for nearly a year, I am still hardly able to distinguish one lunar inhabitant from another, whether it may be a male or a female. Luckily they all wear their names and numbers on their clothes.

When we were within earshot, the ten Tweedledums said, speaking as one man:

"Moo?"

I realised it was a question and supposed that 'moo' meant 'who are you?' or 'what are you?'

"We come from the Earth," I replied.

To my amazement one of the Tweedledums stepped forward and exclaimed in obvious surprise "You speak our Lunatic language! But what is the Earth? We do not have such a word in Lunatic."

I explained as well as I could, with technological interruptions by Tin Pan, that we had landed from our world on the world of the Moon.

"You come here from Boojumania, and you call your land Earth. You are Boojums. We had never thought that Boojums, if they were there at all, would be as lunatised as you seem to be. We have looked much at Boojumania from our great looking-glass and we have thought that if life was there it must be a very poor low life. Have you a great looking-glass on Boojumania?"

"Indeed, we have many," I told him.

"The greatest of which is the telescope erected by the Celestial Chinese Republic in Tibet," Tin Pan said proudly.

"Tibet we do not know. Chinese we do not know. Telescope we do not know. But you have a republic. That is very interesting. You are now in the Lunatic Republic, into which after much fighting for thousands of years all Lunamania has improved itself."

"That is what we hope will ultimately be achieved by the Celestial Chinese Republic," Tin Pan told our Lunatic friend, who asked what we Earthatics called Lunamania.

I explained that there were many names for it, but that in Basic English we called it the Moon. "But the old Romans used to call it 'Luna'," I added.

"How old are they?"

"They have not been there at all for about fifteen hundred years or more, but the Italians still call the Moon 'Luna'."

Our Lunatic friend looked perplexed. "But what are the English and what are the Italians?" he asked.

I tried to explain about our different nationalities.

"That is like us three thousand years ago, before the Abominable War."

"You had a great war?"

"That is why so much of Lunamania is still dead."

"Do you mean to say that terrible desert across a bit of which we tramped after we landed was the result of a war?"

I looked at Tin Pan.

"You had the H-bomb and perhaps even the X-bomb three thousand years ago? I am quite jiggered by what you tell us," the Chinaman exclaimed. And I doubt if that quiet level voice of his had ever betrayed so much feeling.

"What is H-bomb?" our Lunatic friend asked.

Tin Pan had the pleasure of explaining about H-bombs and his own country's much more frightful X-bomb.

"They sound like what we had. When you come to Lunatic City you shall read about the Abominable War," our Lunatic friend promised us. "But I must warn you that it is written in the old alphabet of twenty-six letters. We still use the old alphabet for our personal names except C and Q."

"Ah, yes," I said, "we haven't told each other what our names are. My name is Richard Bosworth and my friend's name is Tin Pan."

"That is quite a Lunatic name. I am called Pup 301.

I have a friend called Tin 42 and another called Pan 844. All names are three letters. Bab 1 to 999, Beb, Bib, Bob, Bub all to 999 and so all through the alphabet to Zuz 999. We do not use mug or wug because we are all mugs or wugs." I guessed that 'mug' was the Lunatic for man and 'wug' the Lunatic for woman, and I was right. Neither 'man' nor 'woman' existed in the Lunatic language. Pup 301 went on talking about names.

"The President of the Lunatic Republic to whom I shall show you when we come to Lunatic City is called Dad 333. Nobody can be born until there is a vacant name for him."

"But how do you prevent that?"

"We have a very strict birth control," Pup 301 replied.

I ought to have said that while we were being given these odds and ends of information about Lunamania we were walking in the direction of Lunatic City, and before I could ask Pup 301 any more about birth control we saw ahead of us a large gate made of some shining white metal I did not recognise and which to his obvious mortification Tin Pan also failed to recognise. Wishing to investigate it more closely, he hurried forward until he was about three yards from it; a moment later poor Tin Pan was stuck to the gate and as helpless as a fly caught on a fly-paper.

"I ought to have warned you not to go so close until I had given the signal to the look-house. Silon is very powerful and must be demagnetised before it is approached," Pup 301 said as he stepped to the side of the road and stood on what looked like the lid of a manhole. Tin Pan was immediately released.

"Silon," the scientist murmured; "we do not have such a metal in the Celestial Chinese Republic."

"It is found in the Great Lunarian Waste, but the mining of it is very difficult on account of the huge hot and cold," Pup 301 informed us. "Many Lunatics had to leave Lunamania before we had enough to make a fence all the length of the Republic."

"Where did they go?" I asked.

"They went into nothing."

I took it he meant they had been killed, and asked why it was necessary to have such a fence. From what was it protecting the inhabitable part of Lunamania?

"It was erected to prevent Lunatics from gazing at Boojumania when it was full, because at such times it was apt to send people mad. These boojumatics, as we called them, became an inconvenience because they believed that they had a right to think for themselves." Tin Pan nodded approval of this condemnation. I felt he was on the verge of addressing Pup 301 as comrade. "But we have doubled our line of look-houses during the last thirty years," Pup 301 added, with a quick glance at Tin Pan and myself. "Ever since you sent fizzers from Boojumania to fall in the Great Lunarian Waste we have been looking very carefully."

As we drew near to the look-house, or guard-house as we should call it, ten Tweedledees came out and saluted our escort of Tweedledums with clenched fists.

Tin Pan's impassivity was not proof against this, and clenching his fist he cried at the top of his not very powerful voice 'Workers of the World Unite!' Then he turned to me. "I shall be more on Earth on the Moon than you will be, Mr Bosworth," he announced with satisfaction.

We were now introduced to all the Tweedledums and Tweedledees in turn, but I was never good at remembering a lot of names, let alone numbers, and the only two that remain in my memory are Xox and Gut. It was later that I kept notes of them.

One might have supposed that the sudden appear-

B

ance from what, by the way, the Lunatics believed was a satellite of theirs would have roused their curiosity to fever pitch. On the contrary, they took us for granted and were not in the least interested to learn what the life of Boojums was like. If Pup 301 or Xox or Gut or any of the rest of them had landed anywhere on Earth they would have been walking about with a perpetual press conference at their heels. Even the fact of our speaking the same language seemed to surprise them very little. At this point I should explain that there are considerable differences between Lunatic speech and the speech of Basic English, but I have a great dislike of phonetics when I am reading, and in relating as well as I can what was said I have abstained from any attempt to reproduce it phonetically; I have also inserted words we use which were not in fact used by the Lunatics. For instance Lunatics always say 'moo' instead of 'who', but I shall use 'who' for the sake of easier reading. When I have finished this brief account of the Lunatic Republic I shall devote my time to a comparative examination of the two languages and as far as I can indicate the Lunatic pronunciation.

"I think you will now be wanting to eat," said Pup 301.

As a matter of fact I still seemed full of bananas and milk from the last two drops of concentrated food with which Heavenly Dragon had been supplied, but I was curious to taste lunar food and we went in to the lookhouse.

I noted at once that like the general tendency all over the temperate zones of the earthly world to erect transparent buildings this lunar guard-house was covered with a material that resembled the new material called clarine developed by the Americans a few years ago as a substitute for glass. The technological gaps in my education to which I alluded earlier compelled me to ask Tin Pan whether it was in fact the same as clarine.

"It is more like the improved clarine which we are now manufacturing in the Celestial Chinese Republic," he informed me, "heat-resisting, cold-resisting and, which American clarine is not, germ-resisting, and we have reason to hope virus-resisting. We shall never again in the Great Prosperity Union of Asia be exposed to false and vulgar Western propaganda about Asiatic plague and Asian influenza."

I realised that Tin Pan did not know any more than I did about this transparent lunar material. I asked Pup 301 what it was called.

"It is called sanaton and it is made out of air. All Lunatics except the President of the Republic live in sanaton hives," he told us.

I observed that he and his fellow-Lunatics obviously did not believe in privacy.

"Privacy?" he repeated. "What does such a word mean? We do not have it in Lunatic."

I explained to him what we meant on Earth by privacy, at which he smiled compassionately.

"We were right to think that you Boojums are very primitive mugs and wugs. Why must you have this privacy as you call it?"

"Well, after all there are one or two motions we wish to perform in private."

And when I spoke frankly of these motions Pup 301 was astounded to learn that we were still at the mercy of functions which had not existed on the Moon since the Abominable War had made uninhabitable all but a comparative fraction of its surface.

"You must be very happy, Bosworth One, to find yourself far away from such a state of body."

I wondered if Pup 301 was right about my state of body. After I had eaten my first lunar meal I found that he was.

When I was a boy I used to hear old people complain about the food they were getting in the middle of the twentieth century compared with what they used to get at the end of the nineteenth century; before everything came out of tins, as they used to say. Well, for the last twenty years I have hardly tasted anything that didn't come out of a tin, and even when I was a small boy I always preferred food that did come out of tins. When my old grandmother used to have me down to stay with her in what we used to call the country in those days I always longed to get back to the tinned fruit and vegetables I enjoyed so much more than the sour fresh fruit and horrible fresh vegetables she used to make me eat. When I tasted my first food on the Moon I felt like telling my Lunatic hosts that they didn't know what food tasted like. Lunar food tastes of absolutely nothing. It is a kind of aggressive nothing like the taste of permanganate of potash when one gargles with it. My plate, which I suppose was made of some kind of plastic, was heaped with what looked like chips of pink cork, and by one of the most formidable efforts of politeness I have ever made I managed to empty it. Tin Pan was less successful.

"You are not yet full, Tin Pan One," said Pup 301 with a hint of reproach in his voice.

"Yes, indeed, I am full," said Tin Pan earnestly, looking at the chips of pink cork on his plate with an expression very different from that of the greedy joy with which children wolf their food in television advertisements.

At this moment a little tray with lavender-coloured pills was passed round and the Lunatics each took one, holding it between his thumb and forefinger. I looked round for a glass of liquid to help my pill on the way down, but I saw none.

Pup 301 held up his hand.

"One, two, three! Chew!" he rapped out in a tone of command, at the same time putting a pill into his own mouth.

I started to chew and was thankful indeed that I still had my own teeth, for false teeth would have been pulled out of my mouth. I remember reflecting as I chewed away laboriously that it must have been the fear of not being able to enjoy chewing gum which had inspired Americans to revere dentistry so highly.

We must have been chewing away for at least five minutes when one of the Lunatics cried 'Chew-hoo! Chew-hoo! Chew-hoo!', at the same time waving his right arm above his bulbish head, and patting his paunch with his left.

"Yid (with some number I have forgotten) has won the chew-chew," said Pup 301. "He is very pleased," he added turning to me. "Next time he will have two vitalots as a prize."

When Pup 301 spoke to me I could not reply at once because my teeth seemed irrevocably stuck together in the vitalot I was trying to chew down. I managed to unwrench them with a faint report. Pup 301 shook a forefinger at me.

"You made a rude noise," he said. "Nobody must go pop in his mouth when he is making chew-chew."

"Not considered good manners, eh?" I commented, balancing that confounded vitalot on my tongue.

"Manners? What are manners?" he asked.

I tried to explain.

"That is what we call rules."

I decided not to ask any more about Lunatic rules at the moment because my vitalot was still pretty active and I was afraid I might go pop in the mouth again.

One by one I saw the Lunatics patting their paunches

to indicate that they had consumed their vitalots.

"You are the last, Bosworth One," said Pup 301.

I looked round and saw the Tweedledums and Tweedledees all sitting upright with complacent Jack Horner expressions on their round blue faces. I didn't mind that, but I was a little annoyed to see that Tin Pan had disposed of his vitalot before me.

"How do you know that Yid did chew up his pill before everybody else?" I asked.

"Because he lifted his arm."

"He might have been cheating."

"Cheating? What is that?"

"It would be cheating if Yid had pretended to have chewed up his pill, but all the time still had a bit of it left in his mouth."

"He could never do a thing like that," Pup 301 affirmed. "That is the kind of thing that the Lunamanians used to do hundreds and hundreds of years ago when mugs and wugs were not equal as they are now."

I felt abashed. Pup 301 quite evidently could not imagine a modern Lunatic cheating.

"It is of course now the same in the Celestial Chinese Republic," Tin Pan put in. "We do not know there what cheating means."

"I question that," I said. "I consider I was cheated over that venusium deal when you threw me into prison."

"That was not cheating. That was for your own good, Mr Bosworth, and to show the rest of the world the mighty achievements of the Celestial Chinese Republic."

I might have been tempted into an argument if Pup 301 had not broken in to ask what venusium was. This gave Tin Pan an opportunity to expatiate on the wonders of the new element which they had discovered in Antarctica.

"This venusium, as you call it," said Pup 301, tapping

his head and smiling, "sounds to me the same as our blankon, the discovery of which three thousand years ago caused the Abominable War between Lunaria and Lunatia. The Lunarians were quite destroyed, but there were enough Lunatians left alive to form the Lunatic Republic and use blankon for their benefit. Yes, I think your venusium must be the same as blankon."

"If we ever get back to Earth, what a lesson we shall be able to teach them, Mr Tin Pan."

Tin Pan did not reply. He was trying to recover the face he felt he had lost when Pup 301 spoke of venusium's antiquity on Lunamania.

"Perhaps you will never go back to Boojumania," said Pup 301. "It has been forbidden here ever since the Abominable War to make any kind of exploration of the sky. If it had not been forbidden to make any more of them we would have lunatised Boojumania three thousand years ago." He lowered his voice as he said 'them'. Then he went on: "Do not look sad, Bosworth One, because Boojums were never lunatised. We shall do our best to lunatise you and Tin Pan One and perhaps Talkery will pass an Action to let you stay with us, even though two more will be added to our numbers than is allowed by the Lunatic Code. And now let us sleep and when the Father of Life rises we will go to Lunatic City."

With this Pup 301 led the way to the dormitory along which were placed twelve beds on either side. My first relief at seeing that they looked just like beds on Earth was rather damped when I found that they were barely four feet long.

"I'm afraid we have no gimper beds in the lookhouse," said Pup 301. "The gimpers are not allowed to come here."

I asked what gimpers were, and I gathered that they

were a special class of Lunatics as tall as myself (and I am a six-footer) whose duty it was to keep the rest of the Lunatic population amused with sport. But I shall have more to say about the gimpers later. The immediate problem was how Tin Pan and I were going to get any sleep for the rest of the night. He was not as tall as I, but he was tall enough to be unpleasantly cramped in a bed the size of a child's cot.

"We must put two beds together," Pup 301 declared, and fortunately this could be managed without depriving any of the rest of the patrol of their beds.

I should have mentioned that Tin Pan and I had divested ourselves of our clumsy protective equipment before we sat down to eat, but when I saw our Lunatic bedfellows stripping for their repose I decided against taking off my own clothes, for I felt sure that I should find I was blue all over and that would have made me give up hope of ever waking from this fantastic dream. So I lay down on the elongated double bed with a pillow under my knees to soften the effect of the two ends sticking up where the beds were joined. Luckily they were quite low.

The toilet made by our Lunatic bedfellows consisted of each one being groomed by and grooming his neighbour in turn with what looked like metal brushes. After this everybody combed his hair, a proceeding which apparently extinguished the luminous hairs. I wondered whether my hair would become luminous after I had lived for a while in Lunamania. I wondered too whether like our Lunatic bedfellows I should presently resemble in one respect a newly born male infant.

And then abruptly I ceased to worry or to wonder and fell fast asleep.

## Chapter 3

I DO not know what time it was on Earth when I woke next morning because I forgot to wind my watch during that ghastly trek from where we landed on the Moon to the frontiers of the Lunatic Republic. Anyway, my watch would not have been of any use for lunar time and it is now in the great Kurarium of Lunatic City, which is the equivalent of what we call a museum, together with my earthly clothes and a picture of my inner self. The Lunatics do not paint portraits of the external individual because every individual looks exactly like every other, and so the art of being able to portray externals has vanished. However, at last a Lunatic painter was found who tried to make portraits of Tin Pan and myself upside down. But I am running ahead too fast and will take an opportunity later on in my account to mention Lunatic art, which to a simple sort of chap like myself seems to reveal the logical conclusion of the way art is going on Earth.

I was saying that my watch would have been no use for lunar time, where A-time begins at the moment when everybody on Lunamania wakes up at the same moment. B-time starts when everybody sits down to First Eat. D-time begins when everybody starts work; C is no longer used in the Lunatic alphabet, its place being taken either by K or S. E-time begins when everybody sits down to Second Eat, F-time when everybody watches the gimpers at their sports, G-time when everybody talks about what they saw in F-time, and H-time when everybody looks at television—the Lunatics call it see-all—which shows what they were doing when they

B*

were working and of course the sport they had watched. At I-time everybody sits down to Third Eat. At J-time everybody can do what he likes, but very few want to do anything except dance until K-time, when everybody goes to sleep until A-time. There is no need for clocks or watches, because everybody knows what time it is.

So when I woke at A-time all the Lunatics jumped out of bed at once and began grooming one another. I felt that Tin Pan and I should have done the same, but both of us were unwilling to strip and I asked him if he thought we might venture to ask for some water.

"I shall enquire of Mr Pup 301 when he has been brushed," Tin Pan said sedately. "But have you seen what a beautiful blue sky is above us, Mr Bosworth? I am so sorry now that I cannot communicate with the Celestial Academy of Science because it is no longer a matter of theory but a matter of fact that the other side of the Moon is inhabited and that the atmosphere here is like a very fine day in the Prosperity Union of Asia."

"Or in the Welfare State of Europe," I put in. "You do not have a monopoly of fine weather."

"We do not wish to have a monopoly of anything, Mr Bosworth."

"Except venusium, Mr Tin Pan," I reminded him.

"We have not abused that monopoly, Mr Bosworth."

"We won't argue about that. However, I don't think you need worry about the failure of communication with the Earth, for I am perfectly sure that nobody on earth would believe what you were telling them about existence here."

"Nevertheless, when we reach Lunatic City I shall do my best to re-establish communication because it is of the highest importance to know that an expedition to the Moon together with the necessary materials to provide for our return is now a perfectly feasible operation."

"Well, my own feeling is that if you do succeed in getting into touch with Earth they'll expect you to return as soon as possible in a flying-saucer, and if you don't do it you'll be condemned for deviation in the first degree. As for me I shall enter the files of S.I.5 as the most serious security risk to the Welfare State of Europe."

"What is S.I.5, please?"

"Spacial Intelligence, Section Five occupies itself with counter-espionage in the sky. They control the spotniks which check up on sputniks and splutterniks and as far as possible on all the people concerned with them. My going off to the Moon will worry S.I.5 a bit."

"But your name was not known," Tin Pan said.

"S.I.5 will soon find out that it was me. However, I'm not worrying. The only thing that's really worrying me just now is how to get hold of some water to clean my teeth. Ah, Pup 301 is dressed now. Let's ask him."

Basic English broke down when it came to asking for water. Pup 301 did not know the word. I tried to explain, but it is extremely difficult to explain what water is when words like 'wet' and 'rain' and 'liquid' and 'moisture' are equally incomprehensible. It was no use my going through the motions of washing; all I was offered was a metal brush. It was no use my trying to signify the act of drinking; all I was offered was a plate of pink cork chips. I was to find out later that there was in fact no water on the Moon. After the Abominable War over three thousand years ago that part of the Moon which had not been destroyed was already depending entirely on nuclear energy. The water from which once upon a time both the Lunarians and the

Lunatians must have developed what I suppose was electricity had begun to get scarcer and scarcer, and a substitute was evolved for the effluence they had produced to provide an atmosphere. I cannot hope to offer a scientific explanation of what happened. All I can say is that, whatever the reason, the fact is that on the Moon drinking of any kind is unknown. One is simply not thirsty. It may seem extraordinary that the bodily needs of Tin Pan and myself were immediately able to adapt themselves to lunar conditions, but the fact remains that they were. Within less than a week I was looking forward to First Eat, Second Eat and Third Eat with pleasurable anticipation, although it always began with those pink cork chips. Moreover, we were soon chewing away at our vitalots as eagerly as the Lunatics, and when the great day came in which I was able to chew up my vitalot before any of the others I was as proud of myself as I should have been on Earth if I had been decorated with the Star of the Welfare State for Civic Service.

After First Eat, which by the way ended with a mauve vitalot much easier to chew than the lavender one of the evening before and therefore not exciting any competition, Pup 301 said the time had come to go to Lunatic City.

"We shall first go to show ourselves to the President, who will perhaps summon Talkery to decide whether we shall make a showabout of you round the Republic. But I must not say any more about matters I am not nearly old enough to discuss."

"How old are you, Pup 301?" I asked.

"I am only ninety-five years old. We cannot be chosen as a Member of Talkery until we are a hundred and twenty-one. Then all of that age draw lots for the vacant places in Talkery."

I asked what was the average length of a Lunatic's life.

"There is no average. Every Lunatic leaves Lunamania when he is a hundred and ninety-nine."

"You mean he dies?"

"That is a very rude word, Bosworth One."

"I beg pardon. But suppose a Lunatic lived longer than a hundred and ninety-nine?"

"When he reaches the age of eternal nothing he is given no more vitalots. So he cannot live longer than a hundred and ninety-nine."

"Do you believe in another life, Pup 301?" He looked puzzled.

"Another life?" he repeated.

"After death?"

"But how can there be life after leaving Lunamania, Bosworth One? We have no room for such life on Lunamania. But I must not talk any more. These are questions you must ask of Dad 333."

"How old is your President?"

"He is now one hundred and fifty-six. The President of the Lunatic Republic is chosen every four years. Any Lunatic M.T. can be chosen by lot for President when he is over one hundred and forty."

I presumed that M.T. meant Member of Talkery, but I did not ask Pup 301 because he was showing signs of slight impatience of these questions of mine and I ceased to probe into the constitution of the Lunatic Republic.

"We must now be going," he told us. Tin Pan and I followed the ten Tweedledums commanded by Pup 301 and left behind us in the look-house the ten Tweedledees. When the latter saw us about to leave their company, they turned round with their backs to us and offered two clenched fists over their shoulders as a parting salute. I thought this was a very practical way of saying good-bye.

Some twenty yards beyond the look-house we came to a couple of wide escalators up one of which we went to reach a moving platform about thirty feet above ground-level, called in Lunatic a self-walk, the four divisions of which were moving in the direction of Lunatic City at different rates of speed from about two to eight miles an hour. Separated from us by a strip of motionless metal was a self-walk going in the other direction. I watched the look-house and the magnetic gate beyond it receding and then gazed with curiosity at the country below, which resembled an immense hop-garden except that it was pink instead of green. The poles too, instead of being wood, were of some kind of magenta metal. Here and there I could see Lunatics obviously engaged upon various tasks of cultivation.

"D-time. Everybody working very hard," said Pup 301. "I am now a lookmug," he added with a touch of complacency in his tone. "I do not work longer to dig the metals we need or to grow the bixifit."

"The bixifit?"

"What you see to give us our eats."

"But you have worked?" I asked.

"Until I was ninety. Now I am lookmug age, and I am pleased. It is more interesting."

"At what age do you start digging for metals and growing this bixifit?"

"When we leave school at twenty. We go to school when we are two. Some draw lots to continue study until they are thirty and after that they will help to manage the Omnibum."

"The Omnibum?" I repeated.

"Where they know all about everything."

"Yes, yes," Tin Pan interjected eagerly. "The

Omnibum is like the Celestial Academy of Science.
Very good. Very good."

"And you were not at the Omnibum, Pup 301?"

"No, I have not drawn the lot to remain at school.
But I do not now regret because if I had not been a lookmug I would not have been the first to see two Boojums
come to Lunamania."

"I notice some roads among the bixifit plantations.
Do you have tractors?"

I had to explain to Pup 301 what tractors were.

"We have self-wagons to distribute the bixifit beans
when they are cut, but we have no self-cars any more
because when everybody in the Republic had a self-car
there came a day when all the self-cars could not move
any more. So we built self-walks to move about and
after that nobody was allowed to have a self-car for
himself."

"Does the power for self-wagons never run out?"

"No, no. How can our power run out?"

"You are not using petrol?"

"What is that?"

"Oil."

"What is that?" he repeated.

I tried to explain; it was useless.

There had evidently never been any oil on the Moon.
I hope if anybody interested in oil reads my account of
Lunamania he will not prospect there for oil, the dis-
covery of which has caused quite enough anxiety for
Earth.

"Why did the self-cars suddenly stop?" I continued.

"Because one day at F-time every road in the
Republic was so thick with self-cars that none of them
could move at all."

"They were in a complete jam?"

"Jam you say when self-cars cannot move? I have a

friend Jam 736. I will tell him when I see him at I-time this evening. He will be very pleased to hear what his name means in Boojumania."

I made up my mind that if I ever did get back to Earth I would do what I could to promote this kind of moving platform. I remember my grandfather telling me about one he had seen nearly a hundred years ago in Paris. The traffic problem in Europe has become an absolute nightmare. In the United Kingdom alone over a thousand people were being killed every week last year, and although it seems a terrible thing to say, I really believe that they were quite pleased about it in Whitehall because it got rid of so many children and old people, and that made things easier for those in charge of education and pensions. During the last five years serious jams have been growing more and more frequent, and one would have thought that the Great Jam of 1994 when two people were starved to death in a sports car before they could be rescued would have led the authorities to do something more drastic than merely pulling down the south side of Piccadilly and Coventry Street, which is after all only one more palliative to get through the next decade. And the country roads! Only a week or so before I left for Peking there was a jam from Doncaster to Stamford which lasted for ten days. Of course, British Railways were delighted and spent £250,000 of the taxpayers' money showing pictures on TV of carefree Diesel trains rattling and bumping along the railway lines at a hundred miles an hour between England and Scotland. But what is the point of dashing from Edinburgh to London in four hours when it takes eight hours to crawl from King's Cross to Kensington? What about the tubes? Well, what about the tubes when fifty people are squashed to death on them every week?

I apologise for this diversion of verbal traffic, but I was thinking of my first sight of Lunatic City, into which from every direction the self-walks were gliding easily along; from these everybody could alight to get on the self-walk that took him to his own hive or workshop or factory.

We must have moved along for at least an hour above those plantations of bixifit, and as the fastest division of the self-walk moved at eight miles an hour and we were walking in the direction of Lunatic City all the while, I suppose that would mean the City was eleven or twelve miles away from the look-house. I am speaking in terms of earthly measurements, for I haven't yet got used to the lunar system, and I doubt if I ever shall. I believe the mighty Einstein himself would have been puzzled by the combination of time and space that the Lunatics call an oop.

"You say there are ten oops from Lunatic City to First Lunatic Town and ten oops to Second Lunatic Town, and then a moment later you tell me that Second Lunatic Town is much further away than First Lunatic Town, but if they are both the same number of oops from Lunatic City how can one of them be further away than the other?"

And as I said, I don't believe that Einstein himself when he was alive would have been able to grasp the answers they used to give to such a question.

Those acres and acres of bixifit over which we were moving became too monotonous after a while and I was glad that we were able to walk and so increase the rate of our progress.

"You have no birds in Lunamania?" I asked.

"What are birds?"

I tried to explain.

"They sound like what we used to call beekilegs.

Once upon a time there were beekilegs, but they were killed in the Abominable War. Not all, but those that remained in what was left of Lunatia were eaten by the Lunatians who survived."

Pup 301 made a grimace.

"It makes us shudder now to think of what the mugs and wugs of three thousand years ago had to do during the years after the War to keep themselves alive."

"We eat birds in the part of the Earth I come from and where Tin Pan comes from, but there are also many people who are vegetarians."

"Vegetarians? What is that?"

"I suppose you are vegetarians here. Bixifit is a vegetable, isn't it?"

Pup 301 shook his head.

"Or perhaps you call it a bush? Or a vine? Or perhaps you call it a shrub? Or a tree?"

But to all of these he shook his head. Later on I was to find that nothing except bixifit grew on the Moon, but whether it can be called a vegetable or not in our sense of the word I do not know. It certainly produces beans six inches across, and the Lunatics call them beans. The pods are at least a yard long and the beans are chopped up in machines before being served. My attempt to depict the vegetation on Earth for Pup 301 was a failure from the start because the colour green does not exist on the Moon. The only colours are pink and blue, with the shades produced by pink and blue—lavender and mauve and lilac. The pink can deepen to purple and the blue can be as rich as twilight. I wish I had put on a green tie before I entered Heavenly Dragon. I think it would have created a sensation and become the most admired object of the public's curiosity among those earthly clothes of mine exhibited in the Kurarium. Unfortunately I was wearing a grey tie when I reached the Moon. Even the greenish-blue of Tin Pan's complexion under the first influence of celestium would have helped a bit, but by the time Pup 301 saw his face it had already turned to that clear Cambridge blue.

Tin Pan himself fidgeted when I was talking about the vegetation of the Earth. He did not think that was nearly as important as the fact of the Chinese having discovered venusium and celestium and, as he considered, thereby showing themselves some way towards being on a level with Lunatic achievement.

"I am impressed, Mr Bosworth, by the advance that these Lunatics have made in Science. I am bound to admit that they have much to teach us," he declared respectfully.

"Will you dare tell them that in Peking if you ever get back there?"

"Yes, it will be my duty to tell them." Then he sighed and sadly shook his head. "But perhaps I never shall go back to Peking. We must not give way to such thoughts," he added firmly. "We must believe that Science is omnipotent. We cannot commit a greater sin than to distrust Science."

While Tin Pan was making his act of faith, the self-walk had passed beyond the great pink expanse of bixifit plantations. Below us now was a network of roads by which trucks at least fifty feet long were travelling, some in the direction of Lunatic City, others away from it. The former were loaded with bixifit beans, the latter were empty. Every road was a one-way road and every truck was moving at the same rate of speed, as far as I could judge at about twenty miles an hour.

"What is the population of Lunatic City?" I asked Pup 301 as I gazed at the immense undulation of gigantic domes of sanaton shimmering in the sunlight but never flashing like glass. Pup 301 then gave me the figures for the population. I have checked these since at the Omnibum. They are as follows: Lunatic City has 455,098 mugs and 455,098 wugs. There are nine Lunatic Towns each with 49,500 mugs and 49,500 wugs. So the population of the Lunatic Republic altogether is 900,598 mugs and 900,598 wugs.

"Exactly the same number of both sexes" I said to Pup 301 when he gave me these figures.

"The same."

"But how do you manage that?"

"If the President approves of your instruction, that is something you can ask the Omnibum. As a lookmug I am not fit to give instruction."

I saw that Pup 301 was beginning to worry whether he had not already gone too far in answering my questions, and I had the tact to refrain from asking him any more. It was not a question of secrecy. The Lunatics were the least secretive people imaginable, but they attached extreme importance to everybody paying attention to his own job, and Pup 301's job as a lookmug was to watch the confines of the Lunatic Republic, not to answer questions about birth control. The arrival of two Boojums at night had prevented him from taking them immediately to Lunatic City, where everybody would have been asleep by the time he could have reached there with them. Now his job was to bring them before the President, who would no doubt summon a meeting of Talkery to decide upon the future of these strangers.

We were now moving along what I supposed was one of the main thoroughfares of Lunatic City, and as I saw the citizens all busily at work on various tasks I realised why Pup 301 had failed to understand what I meant by privacy. The workshops of the Lunatics were covered with that sanaton material which was so much finer than the clarine produced by the Americans.

"And I don't suppose you have anything yet in China to compare with it," I told Tin Pan.

"It is certainly good," he agreed. "But is it germ-proof and virus-proof?"

"I expect so. I can't believe everybody would live to a hundred and ninety-nine if there were any germs about."

"We are now coming to the Management Centre of the Lunatic Republic which is called Pinkhall. All the Management Offices are here, and there is the President's house," Pup 301 continued, pointing as he spoke to a large building at the end of the wide road along which we were moving. "That is the Pink House."

"And it's not transparent," I observed.

"No, the Pink House, the House of Talkery, and the Kurarium are all built of karnicon stone, of which there is only one quarry in the Lunatic Republic."

We left the self-walk by an escalator and passed through a colonnade of what looked like columns of garnet to the front door, on the right of which was a bell which Pup 301 proceeded to toll until the door was opened by a Lunatic well over six feet tall with a long blue beard and a much wrinkled very pale blue face.

"The President will receive you now," said the aged footman.

When we were walking along a corridor to the President's reception room Pup 301 noticed how surprised I was by a kind of Lunatic I had not yet seen.

"When gimpers reach the age of a hundred and twenty," he told me, "they retire from sports. Then for another forty years they teach the gimperlings to run and bound and play feetball. After that for another ten years they become doormugs."

"And then what do they do?"

"Then they leave Lunamania. They remain only for one hundred and seventy years."

"You mean they—" I checked myself in time from using the rude word 'die'. "But why do they not live as long as the other Lunatics?"

"Because they have knocked away twenty-nine years by so much activation."

We had reached the door of the President's shakery, as his reception-room was called. Above it KUMIN was inscribed in that garnet-like metal. It did not strain my ingenuity to recognise this as the simplified-spelling of COME IN.

"Most interesting," Tin Pan murmured. "That is the way we are now proposing to write it in Basic English."

When we entered the room and saw GWOUT above a door at the other end Tin Pan's face fell. In Peking they evidently had not yet thought of GWOUT as a simplification of GO OUT.

The President, who looked exactly like every other Lunatic we had seen so far, was seated on a crimson stool in the middle of the shakery and offered a welcoming hand as we approached.

"You have come here from Boojumania at last," he said, "and you have been a long time coming. We thought you would arrive after that first fizzer reached the Great Lunarian Waste over thirty-five years ago. Sit both."

He indicated two blue stools for Tin Pan and myself to take and turned to Pup 301. "You have done well, Pup 301," he said, "and you have been granted the Pink Star for your behaviour, the youngest Lunatic ever to be given such an honour."

The countenance of the young mug of ninety-five turned to an ultramarine blush, or bloosh in Lunatic.

He went down on one knee and bowed his head in gratitude.

"Dad 333, beloved President of the Everlasting Lunatic Republic, Pup 301 is without words to express his thanks."

"You have also been promoted from second-class lookmug to first-class lookmug and will take up your duties at the Lookalty. And now you can gwout. I have much to ask these Boojums."

Pup 301 turned his back on the President and then bent over to look at him from between his legs a-straddle. I was astonished for a moment, but quickly realised that this was a respectful farewell to the President of the Lunatic Republic. After saluting the President, Pup 301 turned his back on Tin Pan and myself with the Lunatic good-bye gesture of waving his clenched fists at us over his shoulder. I was sorry to see Pup 301 disappear through the door inscribed GWOUT, for I had already become quite attached to him and hoped to enjoy more of his company in the future. However, the important thing at the moment was to make a favourable impression on Dad 333.

## Chapter 4

WHEN we were alone with the President, he looked round the shakery and rising from his stool walked across to a maroon-coloured table and pressed one of a constellation of buttons along the side of it. I could not make out whether the table was metal or made of some plastic substance. Two gimpers with even longer beards than the first doormug came in and were told by the President that he did not wish to be disturbed until he rang.

"We will go now to my chatterbox where only I shall hear what you tell me."

The President led the way to another door in the shakery. Both Tin Pan and I had to bend down in order to follow him into his chatterbox; evidently gimpers were not expected to enter. It was an agreeably cosy room, the walls covered with some pink material which I found out later is woven from the leaves of the bixifit growth. The President pointed to a couple of rocking-chairs and sat himself down in another.

"It was reported to me last night from the look-house that you are called Bosworth One and Tin Pan One. Who is who? The quickspeak did not make that clear."

The quickspeak is the name the Lunatics have for their extremely efficient telephone system. As Tin Pan has not yet been able to find out exactly how it works I shall certainly not make any attempt to explain; I have never yet managed to grasp how an earthly telephone works.

"This is Tin Pan," I said. "And I am Richard Bosworth, the son of John Bosworth."

"You know who your father is?" the President exclaimed in amazement.

"My father is . . ." remembering that 'die' was a rude word, I did not venture to say 'dead'. "My father has passed on."

"And you know who he was," the President repeated to himself. "Then we were right in thinking that Boojums are very primitive people. I suppose you still have wars?"

"The last war was ten years ago . . ." I began, but Tin Pan broke in.

"When in three days the Prosperity Union of Asia defeated the U.S.S.R. We do not think that there will be another war, because the Union of Asia has won the deterrent race."

"I do not understand what you are speaking about, Tin Pan One," the President told him. "But if you can only *think* that there will not be another war we must be very careful in Lunamania. When these fizzers burnt themselves up out in the Great Lunarian Waste we were a little anxious at first, and now since you and Buzworth One . . ."

"Bosworth," I corrected.

"Since you and Bosworth One have come, I am wondering whether we may expect other Boojums. I hope not, because if other Boojums come I fear that you will both have to leave Lunamania."

I realised that leaving Lunamania was a polite way of saying that if another rocket arrived with an earthly passenger list we should not be there to receive them. I am hopeful as I write these words that if any other Boojums do reach the Moon I shall have established after nearly a year as a guest of the Lunatic Republic enough confidence in my hosts for them to allow me to communicate with Earth, that is of course if the next

Boojums who arrive are better equipped than Tin Pan and I were. I do not see any prospect of an expedition arriving with the means to return, for some years to come at any rate. What I am wondering is whether the remarkable way in which my body has been able to adapt itself to lunar conditions means that I shall live as long as the Lunatics. In that case I can surely hope to see Earth again before I reach the allotted lunar span of a hundred and ninety-nine years.

"Yes," I said to the President, "I can easily imagine that our arrival must have been unwelcome."

"No, I do not say that, Bosworth One. Our knowalls will be much interested to hear about life on Booju-mania. Ever since the Abominable War we have refused to allow any experiments in the sky. Three thousand years ago we were in a position to begin our exploration, instead of doing which we turned our know-ledge to destruction. And what I am wondering now is whether you Boojums are going the way we went."

"I will be frank with you, Excellency. . . ."

"Excellency? Why do you call me that, Bosworth One?"

"It is the way we address important people in Boojumania."

"That is very bad for them," said the President. "No Lunatic would venture to believe that he was excellent. The only thing we call excellent in the Everlasting Lunatic Republic is the bixifit which nourishes our bodies and the vitalots which animate them. I am not excellent. I am Dad 333, who by the fortune of the draw am for four years the President of the Lunatic Republic. If you have mugs in Boojumania who consider them-selves entitled to be called excellent they must have puffery. To us puffery is a great offence because a mug with puffery will seek to assert himself over his fellow-mugs. It was puffery which made Lunaria try to destroy Lunatia and Lunatia try to destroy Lunaria, and they would not have done that if so many Lunarians and so many Lunatians had not been puffish among themselves."

"You are right, Dad 333," I assured him, understanding that puffery was the Lunatic for pride.

"That is better," he said, and as his pale blue face crinkled into a benevolent smile I was sharply aware of how appropriately he was called Dad. And then a moment later I was reminding myself that the word 'father' was not used on the Moon except for the Sun, who was called the Father of Life. Nevertheless, it somehow gave me pleasure to address the President as Dad.

"It is true, Dad 333, that we are still near to war in Boojumania, but we have avoided using what you call fizzers and what we call rockets since the Three Days War between two great peoples, called Chinese and Russian, which was a lesson to the Russians they are not likely soon to forget."

"No, no," Tin Pan put in, "they will not."

"I do not understand. What are Russians?" the President asked.

"It is very difficult to speak about Boojumania to people who don't know what it is like and what all these peoples are. You must remember that Boojumania is four times as large as Lunamania and so there is more variety. We have white people and black people and brown people and yellow people and even some red people."

"Yellow people? What colour is that? We don't have such a colour in Lunamania."

"Tin Pan One was yellow until he came here and turned blue. I was white. We have no blue people in Boojumania."

"Did you say you were white, Bosworth One?" the President asked, an expression of dismay, so far as it was possible to have an expression of dismay, on that chubby face of his. "It must have been a great joy for you when you turned blue. White! That is what we Lunatics turn when we say farewell to Lunamania and pass from something into nothing."

I hastily went on before Tin Pan could discourse to the President on the use of white in China for mourning.

"It would take too long, Dad 333, to relate what problems the difference of colour has created for us human beings . . ."

"Human?" the President asked quickly.

"That is what we call ourselves. All mugs and wugs, all men and women as we say, are human beings and the sum total we call humanity."

"As we speak sometimes of lunamanity," the President suggested.

"Exactly."

The President rocked himself quietly in his chair for a full minute without speaking.

"And you do not think that humanity on Boojumania wishes to make war on lunamanity?" he broke the silence to ask.

"I am sure that such an idea has never occurred to any human being. For one thing, nobody believes that there is any life on Lunamania," I replied.

"I can assure you, Comrade President, that none of the great scientists in the Celestial Chinese Republic believes that life exists on Lunamania," Tin Pan put in.

"That is ignorant of them," said the President.

"Yes, but our great scientists cannot see the other side of—of Lunamania from Earth."

"What is Earth?"

"Earth is what we call Boojumania," I put in.

"Yes," said the President, rocking reflectively "it is true that we in the Lunatic Republic cannot see this Earth of yours. Yes, that is true. But if the Earthatics knew that there was such a place as Lunatic City and nine Lunatic Towns, would they try to destroy it with fizzers?"

"Why should they?" I asked, in as passionate a tone of incredulity as I could manage, with the hope that the President really would suppose that human beings were incapable of such wanton destructiveness.

"Yes, but you Boojums are still sending these fizzers into the sky as we did when we were less lunatised than we are now," the President pointed out. "And if you were still trying to destroy one another with fizzers . . ."

"We call them rockets."

"Yes, but that is a rude word in Lunatic. If a mug lets off a rocket in company we pretend not to have heard him. So please do not speak of rockets when you are in the company of Lunatics."

I could well understand that this relic of digestion must be offensive to people who had long ago successfully eliminated all its problems.

"Yes," the President continued, "if you are still trying to destroy yourselves with fizzers how can we be sure that you will not try to destroy us?"

"I can only repeat that such an idea is impossible. Absolutely impossible. We hoped to make war impossible by inventing a . . . er . . . fizzers. They were called deterrents for a long time. And since the Three Days War, though we no longer call them deterrents, nevertheless we still feel that they are deterrents."

"It is indeed sad to hear that people who have the skill to make fizzers should still have the minds of destructive children. Yes, it is very sad," the President sighed.

"When you had the skill to make fizzers three

thousand years ago you must still have had the minds of destructive children to make that ghastly grey wilderness on our side of Lunamania."

"Yes, that is true, but you must agree, Bosworth One, that we learnt our lesson, and it is for that reason I am wondering whether we can let you and Tin Pan One remain in Lunamania. We have had to forbid our Lunatics to go and gaze at Boojumania because when it is full it dazzles the senses and our people used to come back with all sorts of crazy ideas, the most dangerous being the idea that we could build a great fizzer and travel to Boojumania. We did not worry about this so much until these fizzers of yours began to fall in the Great Lunarian Waste; but when they did it became vital for the everlastingness of the Lunatic Republic that we should discourage our people from going to Boojumania because they might have come back with a lot of Boojumatic ideas. And now what security have we that you and Tin Pan One will not be spreading Boojumatic ideas?"

"I shall speak first for myself, Dad 333," I assured him. "I will solemnly pledge myself not to tell any Lunatic how we manage our lives on Earth without first asking permission of yourself or of anybody you authorise to represent you to give some particular piece of information. I pledge myself not to criticise . . ."

"Ah, you have critics still on Boojumania? All critics left Lunamania over a thousand years ago. They were considered flugs."

"Flugs?" I echoed. "What are flugs?"

"We had flugs to plague us until the famous knowall, Pep 5, discovered an invisible vapour which caused all flugs to leave Lunamania and at the same time healed the Lunatics whose creative vitality had been sapped by them."

"But what did a flug resemble?" I asked.

"We know that they were very small blue creatures which attached themselves to mugs and wugs and set up an irritation of the skin and that after Pep 5's discovery of pepsiton they became white before they left Lunamania. Pep 5 was such a benefactor that Talkery decreed after he left Lunamania that no mug or wug should ever again have the name Pep 5."

"Well, what you tell us about critics, Dad 333, makes me more than ever determined not to criticise, and I am sure that Tin Pan One will give the same solemn pledge."

I looked at the Chinese scientist, who bowed.

"I willingly associate myself with what Mr Bosworth One has said, and I am so glad to hear that he accepts one of the fundamental rules of the Celestial Chinese Republic."

"If you decide to let us remain in the Lunatic Republic, Dad 333," I continued, "we shall endeavour to be worthy citizens."

"It will be for Talkery to decide, not me," the President put in.

"There is only one favour I would ask," I said earnestly, "and that is for me to be allowed to study the history of Lunamania in the library of the Omnibum. I wish to write an account of the Everlasting Lunatic Republic, so that if any Boojums do reach Lunamania they can have the advantage of realising at once that they have come to a place which is three thousand years ahead of them. I should of course submit such an account to Lunatic knowalls in order that there may be no mistakes."

The President sat rocking himself for fully five minutes before he replied.

"As I told you, it will be for Talkery to decide, not me, but I am pleased by the way you have spoken,

Bosworth One. However, before I recommend that Talkery should examine the question of your future I wish to hear what my mother thinks about you. No doubt Pup 301 told you something about our system of birth control in the Lunatic Republic?"

"He merely told us that there was a strict system of birth control by which the population was always the same, but he said that he was not qualified to give us any details. He did tell us about the method of nomenclature."

"Nomenclature?"

"The method of allotting names from Bab 1 to Zuz 999."

"Yes," the President said, "and Talkery will have to decide whether two more mugs can be added if there are no vacancies for them. We are so careful in the way we arrange for our wugs to produce muglings and wuglings as needed at the right time."

"And can you arrange for your wugs to produce the right sex?"

"What does that word mean?" the President asked.

I explained to him.

"We do not have that word. If we ever had, it has passed from the language. I am interested because my mother's name is Sex 715. She is going to laugh when I tell her. Yes, yes, long ago we learnt how to give a wug a mugling or a wugling as required. What we have never been able to do, in spite of the many experiments made by our knowalls for the last two thousand years or more, is to produce muglings and wuglings independent of the wug. We have been successful in shortening the carry-time to six months, but only after many years of trying different vitalots, and Gaf 234, a knowall who left Lunamania only last year, was for a long time hopeful of producing a fertilising vitalot which would make the task of wugs completely independent of mugs, but we are still without the secret."

"When it is necessary for wugs to replace the mugs or wugs who will be leaving Lunamania, how are they chosen for the task?" I enquired.

"By lot for the wugs who are thirty years old. I am now a hundred and fifty-six. My mother Sex 715 is a hundred and eighty-six and will be leaving Lunamania in thirteen years' time. And now I shall take you and Tin Pan One to meet my mother."

The President rose from his rocking-chair and led the way to a door on the other side of the chatterbox through which we stooped to pass into a corridor. The walls on either side were hung with pictures of wugs who all looked exactly alike.

"Here are the mothers of bygone Presidents," said Dad 333. "They are kept as examples of old-fashioned painting over a thousand years ago, before our painters began to paint the insides of people instead of the out-sides. My mother is always speaking to have them sent to the Kurarium because one of them is called Sex 715 like herself and she is afraid that when she leaves Luna-mania people will think it is a picture of herself."

We were now ushered by two waitwugs through an anteroom called the sitabout into the bowery to be received by Sex 715, who indeed did look exactly like the portrait of the previous Sex 715 a thousand years ago. Even the costume was the same. It consisted of a pink jacket and a pair of pink plus-fours, but I was interested to see that she wore high-heeled shoes. I was to find out later that the wugs of the Lunatic Republic all wear shoes with similar heels, which bring them up to exactly the same height as that of the mugs. I was also to find out later that only the mothers of Lunatics who are in Talkery or in Management Offices wear pink. All the

C

rest wear blue. The plus-fours are only worn by wugs when they become mothers; until then they wear skirts which do not reach below the knee.

In spite of what we should consider her great age, Sex 715's face was as smooth as a young woman's. Age in Lunamania is revealed by the gradual lightening of the blue complexion. The faces of the muglings and the wuglings are a vivid royal blue; the face of Sex 715 was now the colour of forget-me-not.

"Mother, here are the two Boojums who arrived in Lunatic City this morning."

When I heard the President address Sex 715 as 'mother' my heart gave a leap. It was the first time since we landed on the Moon that I felt Earth still existed.

Sex 715 opened her arms and as it were beckoned us into the circle of her acquaintance. This is the conventional gesture with which wugs acknowledge the introduction of mugs: they never shake hands with them. I feel fairly sure that this must be the relic of a taboo imposed long long ago when artificial insemination became compulsory. Mugs themselves are always shaking hands with one another. If one meets a mug ten minutes after parting with him one always shakes hands with him again: hand-shaking is as much *de rigeur* in the Lunatic Republic as it is in Southern Italy. I was relieved to find they did not go in for the Latin habit of kissing one another. I should certainly have been embarrassed by having to bend down a couple of feet to salute my Lunatic hosts.

When the President's mother opened her arms and made that beckoning gesture neither Tin Pan nor I knew the conventional response to it and we stood there looking rather awkward. The President realised our ignorance of Lunatic manners and laughed. Then he opened his arms less widely and with both of them made a gesture of hurrying into the circle to which he had been invited.

"That is how mugs reply to a wug's greeting," he told us.

Tin Pan and I at once copied his example.

"Very good. Very good," said the President. "You will soon be highly lunatised mugs . . ." he paused a moment . . . "if Talkery agrees that you may both remain in the Lunatic Republic."

"They will agree," said his mother. "And now tell me, Bosworth One and Tin Pan One . . . those are your names I am told . . . what clothes do the wugs of Boojumania wear?" As she asked this question she indicated a couple of rocking-chairs for us to sit in.

At this moment a doormug came in and handed the President a chain of some bright white metal.

"Talkery is now in session," he said. "The decision will soon be made."

With this the President put the chain round his neck and followed the doormug out of his mother's bowery. When we were left in her company she repeated her question about the clothes of the Boojum wugs.

"That is a difficult question to answer," I replied. "As you know, Boojumania is four times as big as Lunamania and in all parts of it our wugs, or as we call them women, wear different clothes. In Tin Pan One's country which is called China many of the wugs wear blue trousers . . ."

"Trousers?" she put in. . . . "What are they?"

I explained as well as I could.

"Ah, yes, I understand. What we wugs call 'forks', and what mugs call 'leggings'."

"And in my country which is called Britain the wugs wear skirts." Again I had to explain the meaning of the word.

"Ah, yes," said Sex 715, "what we call 'spoons'. "That is what our wuglings wear until they are mothers. After that they wear forks like me. But not pink forks. The only wugs who wear pink forks in the Lunatic Republic are those whose sons are M.T.s or chairmugs doing work for the Lunatic Management. All others wear blue forks like the wugs of Tin Pan One."

After this, rather rashly, I tried to explain to the President's mother about fashions in women's clothes. She was much puzzled by this, and yet at the same time evidently intrigued. In fact, I could not help fancying that she was definitely attracted to the notion of fashions. Tin Pan noticed this and said austerely that the women in the Union of Asia did not make themselves ridiculous by following the fashion like the women of the declining West.

"Even the wife of Ba Li-hu, the President of the Celestial Chinese Republic, is always dressed with simple dignity."

"Wife? That is what you call the mother of your President?"

Both Tin Pan and I tried in turn to make Sex 715 understand the difference between a wife and a mother, but she was bewildered."

"You speak of fathers, but we have only one father— the Father of Life."

"We call him the Sun," I said.

"But we have many sons. Dad 333 is my son."

In fact, 'son' in the Lunatic Republic is spelt s-u-n, but I give our spelling for the sake of Boojum readers if I ever have any. I tried to explain the difference in the spelling to the President's mother, but she was inclined to be impatient of our spelling s-o-n.

"Yes, we have always known that Boojums were primitive people and they must certainly be very primitive indeed to spell 'sun' s-o-n. But I still do not understand how what you call a son can be at the same time a father. What is a father? That is what I must know. I feel I am going quite boojumatic myself. Oh, I am sorry. That was not kind of me. You know, when any of our Lunatics goes a little wrong in the head we call him a boojumatic. But I ask again, what is a father?"

I looked at Tin Pan, but he shirked the explanation.

"So the Celestial Academy of Science when faced by an elemental question runs away from the answer," I observed sarcastically. However, in justice to Tin Pan I must confess that I was no more willing to attempt the answer than he was. As a bachelor I have never had to answer the questions of my own children.

"I could explain better what a father means to us if you had marriage, but I understand you have no such institution."

"There is no such word in Lunatic."

"Nor husband."

"That nonsense word is not a Lunatic word," the President's mother declared.

"Nor even wife?"

She shook her head.

I had another shot at explaining about sex, but it is extremely difficult to explain about sex if one is debarred from using the word because the person to whom you are trying to explain it is called Sex 715. However, I must have been successful up to a point because the President's mother suddenly clapped her hands.

"Ah, what you call fathers and husbands are what we call drunes. They have no names; they are all numbers. From 1 to 9999. They live in the Seminary and cost the Republic much to keep them in idleness. Unfortunately they are necessary. It is strange that with our knowall skill we have not been able to propagate with wugs only."

"But how is the number of drunes regulated?" I asked.

"It is easy. All drunes leave Lunamania when they are forty years old. It is not considered wise to use them after that age. So every year some drunes leave and the vacant numbers are filled up by drawing for them as we draw for members of Talkery or for President. What happens then is a secret to wugs, and no wug knows if her mugling is to be made into a drune. From twenty-five to forty a drune does his duty, but if he is a gimper-drune he is allowed ten more years during which he can play hitball. They say that drunes grow tired of existence and often ask to leave Lunamania before they retire from service."

"Do gimper-drunes produce gimpers?"

"Yes, of course. They are fed with special vitalots." The President's mother sighed. "It really is strange," she said, "that when our knowalls have been able to find vitalots to make drunes and gimpers and another to produce a mug or a wug as required, none of them has yet been able to discover a vitalot to make life out of not-life. We had one famous knowall called Zip 456 who analysed the eggs of the bugaboo which had been preserved in the Kurarium, and he was able as he thought to produce artificial bugaboo eggs, but when he injected them with the new vitalot he had discovered the eggs blew up and Zip 456 left Lunamania in a moment."

The voice of the President's mother was grave as she told of that bygone Lunatic martyr to science.

"There were other eggs in the Kurarium, but after that experiment of Zip 456 Talkery passed an Action ordering that all eggs in the Lunatic Republic should be destroyed, and now there is not one. You will be able to see a reconstruction of the bugaboo, and I must tell you, Bosworth One, I am glad they do not exist any longer."

We had been in the bowery for something like an hour, enjoying the conversation of this well-informed and genial wug, a hundred and eighty-six years old, when we heard what sounded like a dinner-bell approaching along the corridor, at which the President's mother clapped her hands in delight.

"You will not now have to leave Lunamania," she said to us. "Dad 333 always rings his bell when he is coming with good news."

At that moment two doormugs opened the door for the President to enter.

"All is well, Mother," he announced. "Talkery has passed an Action allowing our Boojum visitors to remain in the Everlasting Lunatic Republic. I took it as a great compliment to my nuclearity. . . ." I may cut in to explain that 'nuclearity' is the Lunatic word for useful and practical thinking. I wonder how long human beings will have to wait before they can safely allow it the same significance.

"Your nuclearity has always been remarkable, my son, ever since you were first drawn for Talkery," his mother told him. "Was there much talkation?"

"The only question that involved any long talkation was when one of the members from Seventh Lunatic Town proposed that Bosworth One should be known as Boz 1000 and Tin Pan One either as Tin 1000 or Pan 1000. Finally it was decided that they should be known as Bosworth One and Tin Pan One. Members felt that a dangerous precedent would be created by exceeding 999. Moreover, it would seem to imply Lunatic citizenship whereas their status is to be that of Resident Boojums."

"And now," Dad 333 went on as he shook our hands, "we must make arrangements for your beddings and eatings. Let us go back to my chatterbox." As he led the way he stopped to ask his mother whether she thought Tod 51 or Tum 268 was better equipped to show two Boojums the Lunatic way of life.

"They are both sensible young mugs," she replied. "But perhaps Tod 51 is my favourite."

We were to learn later that the sensible young mug called Tod 51 was nearly seventy. Our future guide was not in the Pink House when the President sent a door-mug to summon him, and word was brought that he was away on some Management business in Fourth Lunatic Town.

"It does not matter," the President decided. "If he is not back by F-time you can both come with me to the feetball match between Lunatic City and First Lunatic Town. And you will take Second Eat with me. I will ask one or two prominent Pinks to meet you. And now I shall leave you in my chatterbox until E-time."

## Chapter 5

IT has occurred to me that if any of my fellow-men have reached the Moon and are reading this manuscript of mine I shall perform a useful job by trying to give them a brief history of Lunamania. I fear it will be a sadly amateurish effort because as I have already mentioned I do not possess the technological education to give my account the least scientific value, and history to-day is such a close preserve for specialists that I fear my narrative will not have much practical value. Tin Pan is also working hard at a history of Lunamania, but he is so conscientious about verifying his references that after working for nearly a year now he does not seem able to extricate himself from the drift of paper (riton) with which his blizzard of notes has covered our workroom (ritery) in the Omnibum. If the longevity of the Lunatics is to be achieved by Tin Pan and myself (and in view of the way in which our digestive organs have immediately responded to their diet, I do not see why it should not be achieved), the painstaking Tin Pan may hope to complete his magnum opus within the next hundred years. He is confident of being able to do this and he sometimes talks to me of the posthumous medal he will be awarded by the Celestial Academy of Science if ever any of its members succeed sometime in the distant future in finding the result of his labours. Notwithstanding my lack of a sound scientific education I am able to assert without fear of future contradiction that evolution on the Moon must have been a very much more rapid business than it was on Earth. Clearly if the two great powers Lunaria and Lunatia three thousand years ago had weapons of destruction six

c*

times as powerful as our H-bomb or even this new X-bomb which the Chinese have invented and of which they have retained the secret their civilisation must have been far older than ours. I hazard an opinion that when palaeolithic man was decorating caves with pictures of the woolly rhinoceros the people on the Moon were already sufficiently advanced to be quarreling about religion.

The only sign in the Lunatic Republic to-day that there was ever any religion on the Moon is the name the Lunatics have for the Sun. It may be remembered that the Sun is called the Father of Life and one may notice a slight respect in the tone of the voice when the Father of Life is mentioned.

The religious wars on Lunamania were apparently a struggle between those who worshipped O as the Father of Life and those who worshipped A as the Mother of Life. The people who lived in those parts of Lunamania from which the Earth was not visible resented the cost of pilgrimages to attend the feasts of A (pronounced Ah) because they could not retaliate, O being visible for a fortnight every month from all over Lunamania. For ages both O and A had been worshipped as the Eternal Duplicity, and when Lunatia decided to refuse to worship A any longer on account of the expense, the High Priest of A in Lunaria put a solemn curse upon the Lunatians and was supported by the High Priest of O. This angered the High Priest of O in Lunatia who put a solemn curse on the Lunarians. War broke out and lasted as far as I can make out for at least a couple of centuries, and may have lasted much longer. Naturally those who suffered most from this were the people that lived in central Lunamania, and when I was reading about this war I thought that a kind of parallel could be drawn between it and the

Thirty Years War which was so ruinous to central Europe. In the end there seems to have been just as many worshippers of the Eternal Duplicity as there were of O alone. Indeed, the only positive result apparent is the abolition of A as a name for the Mother of Life in Lunatia and the substitution of Boojumania for it without any maternal attributes. Moreover, in order that superstitious conservatives in Lunatia who persisted in worshipping the Eternal Duplicity should be discouraged the Sun was no longer called O there but was worshipped only as the Father of Life. Gradually through time worship was abolished; the Father of Life was merely accorded reverence, and finally no more than the polite respect, which he receives to-day.

No Lunarian books or manuscripts are in existence to-day and therefore inevitably I have only had access to the Lunatic version of Lunamanian history. Probably the Lunarians had just as many justifiable grievances against the Lunatians as the latter continuously insist they had against the Lunarians. However, even if Lunarian chronicles had been available I should not have been able to read them, their language as far as I can discover from isolated words here and there recorded in the Lunatic chronicles having been quite different from contemporary Lunatic which fortunately for me is so much like English. I have already said that I have deliberately anglicised the method of speech and have used Lunatic words in this account only when the equivalent word in contemporary English or American meant something else or when the Lunatic word had a peculiar flavour of its own.

I feel for instance that if 'Talkery' were substituted for 'Parliament' the average Briton to-day would have a much keener appreciation of what Parliament is worth. The Lunatic use of chatter for conversation is much more expressive of modern conversation. I may mention that 'ch' is spelt 'tz'.

Naturally one of the things I was anxious to know was when water vanished from the Moon, but I cannot find out whether it had already vanished when the Abominable War broke out or whether it was the Abominable War which destroyed what was left of it. Certainly at one time Lunaria was divided from Lunatia by a sea of considerable size, but this must have already shrunk considerably by the time that the great religious war broke out. Indeed, it was the necessity imposed upon the Lunatians of having to travel over-land to worship A whither in former days they had been able to travel in their own floaters, as they called ships, which had made the Lunatians so much embittered against what they began to look upon as the extortion to which they were subjected by the Lunarians. They with that magnificent view of the full and crescent Earth month by month could worship the Mother of Life without having to take a long journey to perform their religious duties. It was interesting to read the attacks of the Lunatian bigots on those who still worshipped the Eternal Duplicity. The doctrine that Lunamania came out of the womb of A without any help from O, from being generally believed became a blasphemous heresy and slowly through the centuries declined into a negligible superstition referred to by Lunatic writers in the same terms as earthly writers refer to the primitive beliefs of savages.

Undoubtedly the growing scarcity of water exercised the ingenious brains of Lunamania for a long while before it finally disappeared altogether, and if the Abominable War did destroy the last vestiges of it the Lunatics who survived were prepared for this eventuality and had already taken scientific measures to discover a substitute.

The same is true about Lunatic independence of the digestive functions. The actual crisis was caused by a scarcity of paper due to the amount of paper that was used in Government offices both in Lunaria and Lunatia. 'Biff', as far as I can make out, was the Lunarian word for what the Lunatians called Government once upon a time; this was changed to Management when the Lunatic Republic was formed. In spite of scientific efforts to provide a stimulus for the rapid growth of trees, the demand on them to supply paper grew continuously with ever more widespread disforestation as a result. At last there were no trees and no paper left at all, and although a suitable substitute was discovered on which official reports could be written, it was too expensive a product to be used for toilet-paper, and laws were passed both in Lunaria and Lunatia making constipation compulsory. At the same time the publication of books was forbidden, and all historical records were preserved in manuscript written, or rather scratched, upon a material called riton which resembles a sort of thick parchment. I do not think that this can ever have been made from the skins of animals, because as far as I can make out there were no animals on the moon by then except certain very large birds which seem to have resembled our ostriches, the last of which were eaten by the Lunatics in their desperate effort to survive after the Abominable War. The situation was saved by the drying up of the sea that used to divide Lunaria from Lunatia, because where the water receded the ground was covered with a pink growth that seems to have resembled lichen. This was discovered to have the property of replacing the digestive functions and was evidently the origin of the bixifit of

to-day, which supports the whole population of the
Lunatic Republic.

The original inspiration for the people of Lunamania
to devote their ingenuity to flying was a desire to get
rid of some enormous monsters called bugaboos which
used to carry people off and devour them. All efforts to
shoot these bugaboos down with the explosive weapons
they possessed proved useless, for some reason which
none of the chronicles I have been able to read explains
clearly, but the importance attached to getting above
these bugaboos before they could be destroyed suggests
that only their backs were vulnerable. At any rate, as
soon as the Lunamanians learnt how to make the equivalent of our aeroplanes the bugaboos, which as far as
I can make out were the only monsters in Lunamania
that flew, had had it, to use a colloquialism. It was no
doubt the development of suitable explosive weapons
to destroy the bugaboos which encouraged the Lunarian
and Lunatian scientists to invent bigger and better
explosives. The early Lunatic chronicles are always
insistent that their motive for this was to provide a
defence against the possibility of being attacked by
Boojumania, and although it may be true that about
this time Daedalus was contemplating the possibility
of aeronautics for the Minoans, with disastrous results
for his son Icarus, we may smile at such fears.

It is permissible to speculate that the threat from
Boojumania was accepted in Lunatia because the
Lunatians could not see our Earth. If they had been
able to rejoice in the sublime spectacle of the full Earth
blazing in blue magnificence every month they would
probably have ridiculed the idea of being attacked by it.
Yet I cannot help thinking that their fear of Boojumania
was really a fear of the Lunaria that in a way could
have seemed an ally of Boojumania. It is noticeable that

references to the Lunarian way of life as something potentially destructive of the Lunatian way of life steadily increase. It is a great pity that no Lunarian chronicles still exist, because it would have been interesting to know if about this time Lunarians were getting equally worried about the threat to them of the Lunatian way of life. I know what the Lunatic way of life is three thousand years after the Abominable War and I can speculate what the Lunatian way of life was, but I cannot find any facts about the Lunarian way of life. The chronicles of the religious wars earlier are so much preoccupied with what may be called the theological arguments about the Eternal Duplicity that they omit to let us know how far the religious beliefs of the Lunarians and the Lunatians influenced their social behaviour. I am inclined to guess that the attitude of the Lunatians in matters of sex may have upset the Lunarians, whose recognition of A as the Mother of Life equal with O the Father of Life may have led them to distrust the rapidly growing practice of artificial insemination in Lunatia. Yet a Lunatian might have argued that the recognition of the mother's greater importance than the father was a more practical expression of reverence for the female aspect of life than the worship of an object in the sky which only existed there by permission of the Father of Life. Be that as it may, the Lunatic chronicles continually refer to the disastrous results of according to the male aspect of life a greater importance or even an equal importance.

I asked some of the Lunatic knowalls in the Omnibum why when the Lunatians rejected the Eternal Duplicity of O and A they had kept the title Father of Life for O. Their reply was that the male principle could not be abolished yet, but they insisted that they were still hopeful of producing life out of not-life, when the difference between mugs and wugs would vanish and the need for maintaining drunes would no longer be a charge upon the Republic.

As far as I can make out, the Abominable War started by accident. For years the Lunarians and the Lunatians kept on inventing more and more powerful weapons of destruction and every knowall who invented a new weapon more powerful than its predecessors was acclaimed as a benefactor of lunamanity because by doing so he had reduced the likelihood of war. The Lunatic chronicles of the past are unanimous in condemning the religious wars as what they call 'unlunatised', but they all agree that lunar nature being what it is the only way to avoid war is to make it too frightful to be contemplated as a solution for any differences between Lunaria and Lunatia. There were of course both Lunarians and Lunatians who argued that the complete destruction of Lunamania was preferable to surrendering to another way of life, but such speeches sound more rhetorical than real when one reads them in the chronicles and the great majority believed that preparation for war was the surest way of averting it. One may speculate that the religious wars earlier had been due as much to a struggle for economic superiority as to any profound religious impulse, but there does not appear to have been any economic cause for the struggle between Lunaria and Lunatia for which both sides were arming. So far as I can make out, neither of the two divisions of Lunamania lacked something which the other part possessed. It is difficult to present a balanced historical account of the causes that led to so disastrous a war when one is still bewildered by an unique experience for an inhabitant of the Earth. However, there has seemed to me during my study of the Lunatic chronicles a faint adumbration of the mental conflict which has divided mankind during the twentieth century and which at the end of it appears to be moving toward a settlement in favour of the mass against the individual, in favour of the ants and the bees against the spider and the earwig. .

My own opinion for what it is worth is that if the Western democracies had gone to war with the U.S.S.R. during the 'sixties victory for the heap and the hive would have been assured whichever side won. That is where I think the anti-pacifists made their grave error. They recognised the inevitability of destruction, but kept on babbling about death being better than slavery. My own belief is that the Russians never had the faintest intention of overrunning Western Europe, which would have been even more of an economic liability to them than it was for the old U.S.A. The fundamental object of the Russians was to keep America from gaining control over the economic future of the East and to achieve that object they took the risk of helping to industrialise China. The result was the Three Days War in which the Russians were as much at the mercy of 700,000,000 resurgent Chinese as once upon a time Russia itself had been at the mercy of Mongolian penetration in search of fresh pastures. What seemed at the time the skilful way in which those running the U.S.S.R. moved all their cities into the vastness of Siberia to render them immune against nuclear warfare from the West made them completely vulnerable from the East. Any hope of the U.S.S.R. being able to recapture the direction of the world from the Union of Asia vanished when the Chinese developed the X-bomb from the new element venusium of which they had an absolute monopoly.

The U.S.A., the United American States of to-day, recognised that they had no future in the East, and now

that they have abandoned the old-fashioned capitalism
to which they clung so obstinately for so long in favour
of social credit the whole of America, North and South,
is enjoying an enviable prosperity.

But suppose a nuclear war had been started forty
years ago, what would humanity be doing to-day? It
would probably be groaning under the insecure and
therefore tyrannical communism promoted by Russia
under an experimental and outdated economic system.
The Earth being so much larger than the Moon it is
improbable that the devastation of a nuclear war would
have been comparable with that inflicted upon the
Moon three thousand years ago, but it is certain that
it would have been widely enough spread to halt the
march of sane progress for many years and make the
survival of the white man as the major influence on the
world's future more than doubtful. It may be true that
without a nuclear war forty years ago the white man's
influence is to-day greatly diminished, but that was
unavoidable from the moment the white man decided
to put himself at the mercy of machinery because from
that moment population was bound ultimately to
become the deciding factor in human power.

The Lunatic chronicles all agree that the Lunarian
threat to lunatisation, as they call it, was the importance
attached to individual prowess, mental or physical, in
Lunaria, but I was unable to discover whether or not
this was the kind of prowess mankind still admired not
so long ago. We all despise it now, of course, though
many of us in our own hearts still retain a sentimental
respect for it. The much more rapid evolution of the
Moon compared with earthly evolution makes it
impossible for a human mind to appreciate what life
was like here three thousand years ago. Involuntarily
one begins to think of those Lunarians and Lunatians as

like the Greeks and Trojans of long ago, and that makes nonsense. Nevertheless, as I said just now, I do seem to discover in the mutual hostility of the Lunarians and Lunatians a nebulous foreshadowing of the struggle for the future of man in the latter part of this twentieth century. It is clear that when the Abominable War broke out the Lunatians were already tending toward the development they have now attained in the Lunatic Republic, where they are completely satisfied with their condition and where naturally the enemies of that development three millenniums ago were presented as malific forces overcome at last but even now unforgiven.

The horror of that war must have been beyond anything even faintly comparable with what we on Earth have endured. Apparently it began by an accident, though of course the Lunatic chronicles insist that the accident was deliberately planned by the Lunarians. A Lunarian 'zoomer' and a Lunatian 'zoomer' crashed into one another and both 'zoomers' dropped and exploded. Zoomer is the Lunatic word for something like what we call a bomber: I cannot find what the Lunarian word was. This first explosion was the signal for what we call guided missiles on both sides to be let off. The Lunatic name for guided missile to-day is 'fizzer', but the earliest chronicles refer to them as 'krushers'. I have not been able to establish how long the war lasted; it obviously did not take much time to turn practically the whole of Lunamania into the ghastly waste it is to-day. At the end of it not a vestige of Lunaria remained and of Lunatia only a comparatively small fragment. The struggle of those Lunatians left to survive was appalling, but somehow they did survive. The memory of Lunatia was too painful, and one of the first steps the Lunatians took was to form themselves into the Lunatic Republic which, with what at the time must have seemed a rash challenge to the future, they called the Everlasting Lunatic Republic. Lunatia became a forbidden word to use; it does not appear after the earliest of the Lunatic chronicles written a few years after the Abominable War.

The chroniclers claim, probably with justice, that the only way to preserve the life of those left in Lunamania was to achieve a corporate mind whose decisions were absolute for all the component parts of it. The need for every Lunatic to work for the preservation of the Republic made it necessary to remove from him any desire to indulge in emotions that might interfere with his work. Artificial insemination had been growing as a custom in old Lunatia and one of the things that the Lunatians held against the Lunarians was the opposition of the latter to artificial insemination. This was now made compulsory in the Lunatic Republic, and the penalty for practising any other method of propagation was banishment to the Great Lunarian Waste, which meant being frizzled or frozen to death according as the culprit found himself there by day or by night.

I have mentioned the final solution of the food problem by the appearance of that pink growth after the drying up of the sea between the two sides of the Moon, but the description of what the Lunatics had to endure for awhile in their efforts to keep themselves alive is too unpleasant, too disgusting and gruesome indeed, to dwell on.

It would be rash to attempt from a study of the Lunatic chronicles any forecast about what humanity will be like three thousand years hence, because it is impossible to discover how nearly the mental attitude of the lunar world three thousand years ago approximated to ours of to-day. Furthermore, it is impossible to estimate for how many years before the Abominable

War the lunar world had emerged from primeval savagery. The utter destruction of the past has allowed the post-war Lunatics to present that past in a light entirely favourable to themselves. Suppose that on the Earth to-day a comparable destruction of much more than half the world took place and all that remained was a piece of Russia or a piece of China would a Lunatic landing on Earth be able to form any notion of earthly history, let alone pre-history? No; he would be dependent on a work like the Russian encyclopaedia or the great Chinese encyclopaedia which is now being published, in both of which historical figures and facts have shrunk to the size which is consistent with the way of life to which it is desired to accord infallibility.

I am under the impression that the material progress of humanity to-day is still many hundreds of years behind what had been achieved in the lunar world when the Abominable War almost utterly destroyed it. Nevertheless, my experience of the Lunatic Republic fills me with apprehension for the future of humanity because humanity seems to be moving in the same direction.

The oldest man I happen to know on the Earth is a Briton born in 1899 who fought during the last two years of what was called for a short time the Great War for Civilisation. His mind is clear and his memory of the past remarkable. When he speaks of God I am unable to avoid an uncomfortable feeling that he may be right and that, although we have forsaken God, God Himself has not forsaken us. I would give much to be able to return from this strange experience and tell that old man about the Lunatics. I think he would probably declare that the Lunatics are without souls and then I should ask him if his theological dogmas allowed him to believe that God could deprive human beings of their souls. I wonder what his answer would be, and as I write these words I am filled with an inexpressible longing for the sight of greenery again and the feel of water. What would I not give to be able to return to Earth and tell them what the Lunatic Republic is like? But alas, with the present direction that humanity is taking I might find that instead of providing a warning I was providing a desirable example which would encourage humanity to press on all the more urgently along the road it has taken.

In none of the Lunatic chronicles is there any hint of such a belief in God as was held by the whole of humanity in some form or another. The argument about the comparative importance of O and A as the authors of life, which provoked the religious wars in Luna-mania, is nowhere set forth clearly by the Lunatic chroniclers, who treat these wars as an attempt by Lunaria to score off Lunatia for which the Eternal Duplicity was merely a pretentious excuse. Nevertheless, the fact that even to-day the faint respect in the voice of a Lunatic when he refers to the Father of Life does suggest an admission that something exists beyond their comprehension, though I am well aware with what contemptuous superiority any of my Lunatic acquaintances would deny such a suggestion. It must be remembered, however, that only the Lunatic point of view has been preserved. The Lunarians with their way of life and habit of thought have vanished from recorded history, and not even a dim shadow of them endures in legend. On earth the Catholic Church, unaccountably as it appears to many of us, still exercises as much power over the minds of many millions of human beings as ever, and although the Orthodox Church seems to have surrendered to a political idea and the various Protestant sects, in spite of achieving a kind of expedient unity, show an ever-growing decline of influence, the Godless humanitarianism which controls the world economically, politically and socially is still pathetically nervous of that religious revival which it would try to stamp out as a reactionary plot.

I fear that my divagation into Lunamanian history has not been a profitable exercise, amounting as it does to not much more than surmise. However, I felt such a divagation was necessary because it stresses the value of history. The Lunatics dependent upon the presentation of facts made to fit in with a master theory are without history; the result of that is all too evident in their present condition.

Moreover, philology is wanting. I am faced by the surprising existence of a kind of Basic English, but I cannot discover whether there was ever any other basic language in Lunamania. I remember my father telling me when a boy about some story he had read at school in Herodotus—I never learned Greek myself—in which some king or other wanted to find out what was the original language of mankind. So he put two babies with a mute nurse on a desert island and the first word they spoke to the investigator who was sent by the king to report on his experiment was the Greek word for bread, thus proving to the satisfaction of the enquiring king that Greek was the original language of man. Now it would be ridiculous to argue that English was the natural language of man, but the fact that Basic English is now coming to be accepted all over the world as the easiest form of communication may be an indication of what happened on the Moon long long ago. Anyway, however it came about, English is what the Lunatics speak, though I must remind any at present unimaginable reader of my account that I have deliberately made the Lunatic form of English easier for him to follow than it would be if I tried to do it phonetically. If I had done that, my unimaginable reader would have as little idea of what Lunatic sounded like as anybody ignorant of Cockney would have after reading Bernard Shaw's absurd attempts to reproduce it phonetically in his plays. For me to write Lunatik Republik and substitute an 's' for every soft 'c' would become tiresome.

Well, while my unimaginable reader has been finding himself as ignorant of Lunamanian history as he was when he started upon my digression, the President has completed his business and has invited Tin Pan and myself to join him at Second Eat.

## Chapter 6

THE Small Eat Room at the Pink House, so called in distinction from the Big Eat Room in which the state banquets were held, was like the inside of a vivid magenta hemisphere. I found later that magenta was used everywhere in the Lunatic Republic for eat rooms because magenta was considered an encouragement to appetite. We know that in the Victorian era red was the favourite colour for dining-rooms; I wonder if this was at all responsible for the enormous meals which we are told the Victorians consumed. Besides being always magenta-coloured, the eat rooms in the Lunatic Republic are always circular, that shape also being held conducive to appetite. The eat table was round too, and also the stools on which we sat. Tin Pan being shorter was not so much incommoded as I was by the lowness of his stool, but my legs got into a tangle, and the President, noticing my difficulty, asked if I would like a blow out. At first I thought he was enquiring about my appetite, but soon realised that he was asking me if I would like an air-cushion instead of a stool, and a waitwug was sent to fetch one for me.

The two waitwugs in attendance did not serve the food. The plates of bixifit came down through the ceiling suspended from five silvery chains that unhooked themselves immediately and went back through the apertures in the ceiling, which closed again. Nobody spoke while we ate our pink chips. This was done with what looked like plastic spoons for which the Lunatic name is 'spade'; 'spoon', it may be remembered, is the Lunatic word for a wug's skirt.

I noticed that Tin Pan was getting through his bixifit much faster than at Third Eat the evening before, or First Eat this morning, and I must add that already he was acquiring a Lunatic appetite. When the bixifit was finished, the apertures in the ceiling opened and the silvery chains came down to pick up the empty plates and remove them through the ceiling. Then a circular disc in the middle of the table dropped and came up again with a plate of lilac-coloured vitalots, each of the eaters taking one and holding it between his forefinger and thumb until the President said 'One, two, three, chew!' and immediately popped a vitalot into his own mouth. However, on this occasion there was no competition to finish one's vitalot first, and it was the President who after looking round said 'Chew-hoo'. It seemed to be a kind of grace to which the guests responded by putting their hands on either side of their heads and waggling them about. I am always quick to do in Rome as Rome does and flapped away like the rest, but Tin Pan with his more conservative Chinese nature could not bring himself to make this gesture until he was perfectly sure that he could do it properly.

"And now we will sit awhile in my chatterbox before we go to see the feetball at F-time."

Tin Pan and I were presented to the three prominent Pinks whom the President had invited to meet us.

"This is Jaz 119, the Talkeroon of Talkery."

I presumed that Jaz 119 must be the equivalent of our Speaker.

"This is Cod 678, the First Look of the Lookalty."

I knew from Pup 301 that the Lookalty was an important Management Office of the Lunatic Republic, the equivalent of our Ministry of Defence. I felt inclined to say that in Britain we used to have a First Lord of the Admiralty until his office was incorporated in that of the Minister of Defence, but decided, remembering the difficulty I had had in trying to explain to Pup 301 what water was, to abstain from talking about ships. I had not yet begun my reading of the Lunatic chronicles and therein learned about the floaters of three thousand years ago.

"And this is Bum 444, who is in charge of Gimpery."

By now I was able to make the Lunatic acknowledgment of an introduction without the least embarrassment, and I was glad to notice that Tin Pan was already yielding to the social conventions of the Lunatic Republic. I do not offer any description of these prominent Pinks because outwardly they were all exactly like any other mug in the Lunatic Republic.

"In Boojumania," I observed to Jaz 119, "jazz is the name of an old-fashioned kind of music and dancing to jazz was extremely popular until it was displaced by another old-fashioned kind of music and dancing called rock 'n' roll."

"Ah," said the Talkeroon, "my writemug is Rok 909. You must show us how to dance jaz and rok when we dance at J-time."

"I'm afraid my dancing days are over," I demurred. "I'm too old for dancing."

"But one is never too old to dance," Bum 444 said with a broad smile. Then he turned to the rest of the company: "Our friend Bosworth One, who says he is only fifty years old in Boojumania, has just told me that he is too old to dance."

The President and the other two prominent Pinks laughed uproariously at this announcement, and I tried to change the subject by telling Bum 444 that our word for 'ritemug' was 'secketary'.

"It used to be 'secretary', but the announcers of news on what we call television and you call 'see-all' found

it difficult to pronounce and so it was changed to
'secketary' by the International Directorate of Basic
English in Delhi."

Tin Pan nodded his head in grave endorsement of my
statement.

"The delegates of the Celestial Chinese Republic
being in favour of 'secletaly'," he added, "but as always
desiring a peaceful settlement they were willing to
withdraw their objection."

It was obvious that our Lunatic hosts were not in the
least interested in our information about the domestic
life of Basic English, and Bum 444 cut in to ask what his
name meant in Boojumania.

"I'm afraid it means a useless kind of mug," I said
apologetically.

"A useless kind of mug?" Bum 444 repeated in
obvious astonishment. "But do you allow useless mugs
to remain in Boojumania?"

"We are gradually getting rid of them in labour
camps, but there are still quite a number of them
bumming around as we say."

"It appears that the Boojums are indeed in a more
primitive state than we supposed," said Jaz 119. "I think
Cod 678 will have to bring before Talkery the question
of replying to these fizzers which they have been shooting into the Great Lunarian Waste for the last thirty
years and more. If useless mugs are still allowed to
exist, they may obtain power and try to attack Lunamania."

"Oh, there is no likelihood of that," I said hurriedly;
but I could see that my revelation of useless people still
being allowed to exist on Earth had seriously perturbed
our Lunatic hosts.

"Do not imagine that the fizzers which have been
landing from time to time on Lunamania have any

hostile significance," Tin Pan insisted. "The Celestial Chinese Republic is determined to promote not merely peace on what we call Earth but peace in what we call the Universe."

"The Universe?" Cod 678 asked.

"Of which the Earth and the Moon—Boojumania and Lunamania—are a part," Tin Pan replied.

"Yes, yes," the President put in, "I understand. We call it the Tote. But why do the Boojums send these fizzers to us?"

"Because they provide us with valuable information about the atmospheric conditions of Lunamania," I told him.

"From which we had hoped to profit when Mr Bosworth—Bosworth One I mean—and myself were the first human beings—the first Boojums I mean—to land on the—on Lunamania," Tin Pan explained. "Unfortunately our communication system failed to work, and at this moment nobody in Boojumania knows whether Mr Bosworth One and I have arrived or not."

"It is better that they do not know," the President declared firmly.

"Much better," the three Pinks agreed.

"It may be, of course," the President went on, "that other Boojums will arrive, in which case Talkery will decide how they will be treated. Meanwhile, you will both be granted the full hospitality of the Everlasting Lunatic Republic until the time comes for you to leave Lunamania a hundred and forty-nine years hence."

"I must remind you, Dad 333," I said, "that although Tin Pan One and I are very young at fifty by Lunatic standards we are considered in Boojumania to be middle-aged, which is what a Lunatic would be when he was about a hundred and fifty. So we are not likely to trespass on your hospitality for more than another half century or even as long. On the other hand, your wonderful methods of nutrition with bixifit and vitalots may allow us to be here longer."

"We shall see," said the President. With a twinkle in his benevolent eyes he added, "But I think I shall be leaving Lunamania before you do—unless more Boojums arrive, and then I cannot answer for what Talkery will decide. But come, it will soon be F-time and we must be going to the gimpasium. You are lucky. A feetball match between Lunatic City and First Lunatic Town is always a big occasion."

The President led the way to the entrance of the Pink House, and thence to the self-walk, which was thronged with passengers who after they had greeted their President with an affectionately respectful salute could not refrain from staring at Tin Pan and myself.

"Your arrival in Lunamania and the decision of Talkery to accord you the full hospitality of the Lunatic Republic was announced by the Chief Bigmouth at E-time and it is natural that the people will be gazing at you for some time to come. You must not resent it. I am sure that if the Talkeroon and I arrived on Boojumania the Boojums would all stare at us."

I was on the verge of saying that as Tin Pan and myself had turned blue when we reached Lunamania they would probably turn white, when I remembered the uncomfortable significance of such a change in Lunamania and bit back the remark in time.

"Tin Pan and I shall expect to be gazed at for a long time to come," I said. "But what is the Chief Bigmouth, Dad 333?"

"The Chief Bigmouth is a mug, not a thing. He is Manager of the Office of Announcement which we passed a few moments ago in Pinkhall. His duty and that of the bigmouths under him is to make public statements over the hear-all, and when a particularly important statement has to be made the Chief Big-mouth makes it himself. Nine bells are struck first, and this is a sign to the people that they must pay special attention to the statement. Though, of course," the President continued hastily, "the people all pay attention even if it is only a wun bell statement."

I have spelt 'one' as the Lunatics spell it. How the knowalls at the Omnibum laughed when I told them the way we spelt 'wun' in Boojumania!

By now the self-walks from every direction were approaching the gimpasium, but there was no con-fusion as the throngs of spectators entered the huge arena by forty different escalators. For us in the President's party there was a special escalator by which we descended into the President's box, or, as it was called in Lunatic, the President's peepery.

"This is larger than our new youth stadium in Peking," Tin Pan murmured to me in awed voice.

"It certainly is. How many spectators can you accommodate?" I asked him.

"A quarter of a million," he said proudly.

"Well, I've just asked Bum 444 how many the gimpasium can accommodate and he tells me that it holds three-quarters of a million. Good lord, this vast pink expanse makes Wembley look like a billiard table."

Indeed, it was a truly terrifying spectacle. I reckoned that the arena, which in Lunatic is called the ballroom, was about half a mile long and a quarter of a mile wide and all round this expanse of what I can best describe as resilient pink cement were tiers of benches rising to a height of at least six hundred feet, the myriads of onlookers seated on them dressed in blue and all with blue faces giving the effect of a heaving cloud of blue. The stands on either side of the President's peepery were reserved for Management officials, who like their mothers were all in pink of a slightly darker shade than the ballroom. The peepery itself was about fifty feet above the ballroom and we who were privileged to be in it were all seated on rocking-chairs. On other occasions when I attended sporting events, and had to sit on a bench designed to seat people only four feet high, I found it rather uncomfortable for my long legs.

Before the game started the President suggested that Bum 444, the Manager of Gimpery, should tell me something about it, and I learned from him that every mugling who is born even a second or two after the carry-time of six months is registered for examination three months later with a view to selecting him for treatment with the vitalot which causes him to grow to a height of six feet and sometimes even an inch or two over. The number of gimpers is nineteen hundred and ninety-nine, and the number of gimperlings is regulated to maintain this number. Gimpers have no names and are drawn by lot, but the names they received when born are entered in the records and are not given to other muglings or wuglings until the gimpers leave Lunamania when they reach the age of a hundred and seventy. The loss of twenty-nine years of the normal life of a Lunatic is due as already mentioned to their years of what is called activation. They appear as fully trained gimpers at the age of forty and perform until they are a hundred and twenty. Then they become trainers for another forty years and spend another ten years as doormugs until they leave Lunamania.

A gimper is expected to be an all-round athlete, but specialisation is permitted after he is fifty. However, this is strictly watched by the Management of Gimpery and if there is any sign of the spectators indulging in what is called personalifikation a gimper is debarred from performing in what he excels. A wrestler, for which the Lunatic word is 'squeezer', who finds himself the object of too much attention is likely to be put back in one of the feetball teams. In grave cases of personalifikation a squeezer or a kikwik (the word for boxer) may find himself publicly humiliated by being made to run a race in which he cannot help being the last.

I asked Bum 444 how without a name a gimper who looked exactly like the next gimper could impress his personality on the spectators.

"He has a number," said Bum 444. "Personalifikation may affect a number as harmfully as a name."

I asked where the gimpers lived.

"Nine hundred and ninety-nine live here in the great gimpasium of Lunatic City and ninety-nine live in each of the gimpasiums of the nine Lunatic Towns. The other gimpers are attached to Gimpery, where we employ them on various matters connected with the Management. Gimpers are not allowed by the Lunatic code to eat or talk with ordinary mugs and wugs with one exception. When the time draws near for a wug to be drunified she is encouraged to dance with a gimper at J-time because our knowalls have found that such activation puts her in the most favourable state for drunifikation. Experiments have been made with different vitalots to avoid what we consider a regrettable survival from ancient times, but no vitalot has yet been discovered as effective for a wug about to be drunified as dancing with a gimper."

"Yes, I can imagine that," I murmured gently to myself, and a moment later there was a roar from the myriads of spectators to greet the appearance of the teams on the ballroom, twenty-five in each side. The Lunatic City gimpers wore magenta shirts with pale blue sleeves and pale blue shorts; the First Lunatic

D

Town gimpers were in royal blue shirts and carmine shorts. Instead of stockings they were all in boots of a deep purple hue that came about half-way up the blue calves of their legs. The goals at either end of the ballroom consisted of three circles on top of one another, each circle being about a couple of yards in diameter. Five points were scored for kicking the ball through the bottom circle, two for the middle circle, and one point for the top circle. I was soon to realise the reason for an apparently illogical system of scoring because it seemed to me that the top circle must be the most difficult. In the middle of the ballroom was a rectangular goal rather smaller than the regulation socker goal, and the ball had to be kicked through this before either side could attempt to tackle the circle goal at either end. The rectangular goal was defended by three goalkeepers on either side standing back to back but not allowed to use their hands. The Lunatics do not use the word goal; they call the two circle goals 'endbuts' and the rectangular goal in the middle of the ballroom the 'passbut' and it will be simpler to follow the game if I use the Lunatic nomenclature.

"You will now excuse me, please, for a few minutes," said Bum 444, "because at this match it is always the custom for the Manager of Gimpery to set the ball."

A gimper from the Management now presented himself carrying a purple ball at least six times as large as a socker ball with which he preceded the Manager of Gimpery down the escalator from the President's peepery to the accompaniment of a roar that made the noise of any roar in an earthly stadium sound like a gurgle.

"Bum 444 is a First Town mug," said the President, turning to me with a smile," and he is hoping now that First Lunatic Town will win to-day, but I think they will find it hard to beat Lunatic City."

The Manager of Gimpery soon reached the passbut, and taking the ball from the attendant gimper he placed it almost reverently, not as I expected on the ground in the middle of the passbut, but on the top of the crossbar. Then suddenly he came back to the peepery in a series of bounds, each about ten feet high. I was staggered.

The President seeing my amazement explained that the keepdown had been turned off for play to begin.

"The keepdown?" I repeated.

"Ah, you have discovered a way to apply gravity," said Tin Pan. "I have been much puzzled since we arrived in Lunamania to find that when we came out of the Great Lunarian Waste we were able to get rid of our weighted equipment."

"The keepdown was discovered many thousands of years ago," said the President. "But we find it much better for feetball as a game to allow the players the greatest freedom of activation."

"It may be one of the heavy gases that we surmise exist in the depths of the Moon," Tin Pan muttered to himself. He did not elaborate his theory, for by now he regarded me as such a hopeless ignoramus over chemistry and the rest of it that he could not be bothered to instruct me about what he considered were facts so elementary that my ignorance of them made the prospect of ever attaining to a real appreciation of science infinitely remote.

"But if you have turned off the keepdown, how can the spectators keep their seats?" As I asked this question I could not resist giving Tin Pan a triumphant wink to claim that I was not quite such a nitwit as he thought me.

"The keepdown is only turned off from the ballroom. We are quite as usual here."

And as he spoke Bum 444 followed by his attendant

gimper alighted upon the escalator and walked sedately into the peepery.

"You don't have a referee or touch-judges, I notice," I said to him.

"What are such things, Bosworth One?"

I explained about our referees and touch-judges at football, and he was obviously shocked.

"But no gimper in the Lunatic Republic could break the rules of feetball. Nobody in the Lunatic Republic could break a rule about anything," he declared.

I remembered how shocked Pup 301 had been when I asked him about cheating at chew-chew, and made a mental note never to mention this subject again in case I might be suspected of corrupting the morals of the Lunatics.

When the Manager of Gimpery had left the ballroom the players stood with their arms stretched above their heads in the attitude of divers until a sharp whistle sounded, when what we should call the forwards bounded into the air to dislodge the ball above the passbut. Amid delirious shouts from the supporters of First Lunatic Town this was achieved by one of their gimpers, who kicked the ball back for another Town gimper to kick the ball through the passbut and thus allow the whole side to press forward to attack the City endbut.

I am bound to say that I have never found any earthly football anything like as exhilarating to watch as this Lunatic feetball. The players hardly seemed to touch the ground at all and I now realised why the lowest circle of the endbut counted five points, for the ball which I had supposed would be too heavy to kick high seemed to float about like a balloon. I saw one kick by a Town back which must have sent the ball at least three hundred yards.

After twenty minutes, during which there had been no score, the whistle sounded for first time, and apparently the keepdown was turned on while the gimper trainers came on the ballroom with vitalots for the players. While these were being chewed, cheer-leaders from Lunatic City and First Lunatic Town marched up and down in front of the stands, doing what resembled the rock 'n' roll of my youth to the accompaniment of what looked like large lyres.

I asked Bum 444 how long the game would last.

"Four times of twenty minutes."

At this moment the whistle blew again for play to recommence, and the ball having been placed on the crossbar of the passbut by one of the gimpers during the interval the bounding and kicking of the fifty players began again. There was no score during second time and none during third time, and the spectators by now were in a long roar of excitement, which reached frenzy when a couple of hundred City mugs and a couple of hundred Town mugs took the place of the cheer-leaders, and when the keepdown was turned off started to leap up and down along the touch-lines on both sides of the ground, yelling exhortations to the gimpers. And when I say 'started to leap up and down' you must realise that they were leaping ten and sometimes even fifteen feet into the air. It may be asked why if ordinary mugs could jump like this they left the playing of games and the athletic contests to gimpers, and were themselves only content to watch. When I say that the record for the Lunatic high jump was made two centuries ago by an Eighth Town gimper who cleared 31 feet 2 nails (inches) and the record long jump was made as lately as forty years ago when a Fourth Town gimper achieved 112 feet 9 nails, it will be realised that for a few active mugs to bound fifteen feet into the air in the excitement of a toughly contested match would not have been deemed worth watching as an exhibition of jumping. Incidentally, the Lunatics do not speak of jumping; they call it bounding.

It was within two minutes of time that a First Town gimper put the ball through the top circle of the City endbut: First Lunatic Town had defeated Lunatic City by one point to nil when the whistle blew. The delight of Bum 444 was a pleasure to see, and later the President and the First Look of the Lookalty, who were both Lunatic City mugs, and the Talkeroon who was a Third Town mug, were all obviously glad that Bum 444's service as Manager of Gimpery should have been marked by this notable and unexpected triumph.

"I will congratulate the leader of the First Lunatic Town team," the President announced, "and I will condole with the leader of the Lunatic City team," he added. "Let them both come to the peepery while the hivers are leaving the gimpasium." Hivers, I should explain, is the word for people.

"They will both be very glad for that, Dad 333," said the Manager of Gimpery, beaming as he went down the escalator to fetch the two gimpers.

It was touching to see the paunchy little President just four feet tall making the gesture of welcome to the two gimpers, both of whom stood well over six feet, and even more touching to see the gimpers give the answering gesture of hurrying into the hospitality of the President's arms.

"Gimper 1805 of First Lunatic Town," said the Manager of Gimpery.

"I give you my congratulations," said the President. "And I send my congratulations to the twenty-four gimpers who have given to us all such a very good game."

"And this is Gimper 1689 of Lunatic City," the Manager said.

"You have been very sportful losers," said the President, "and we have all enjoyed the good game you gave us."

The two gimpers turned round and bent down to salute the President with clenched fists through their legs a-straddle. Then they retired from the peepery.

"There is no sign of personalifikation in Gimper 1805," the President observed.

"None whatever," Bum 444 eagerly agreed. "Our Gimpery officer in First Town would notify me at once of such a development. Of course, there will be a good deal of excitement at chatter-time and when see-all starts in First Town at H-time that excitement will be doubled but I feel that First Town hivers will have the right to rejoice. Do you think I might authorise an issue of vitalot 12 at Third Eat this evening in First Lunatic Town?"

"I think it would be very suitable," said the President. "Our friend Bosworth One looks at me with a question in his face. You shall have a vitalot 12 yourself at Third Eat. And that reminds me. We must be getting back to the Pink House because Tod 51 will have to make arrangements for our guests. He can call on Gimpery to supply two gimper beds, I hope."

"That will be arranged," said Bum 444.

"You know, it has occurred to me, Dad 333," said the First Look, "that it would be useful if we could have a gimper attached to each of our look-houses so that if these Boojum fizzers fall near by we can get a report more quickly than we could by sending out a chunk (patrol) of lookmugs."

"That's a very stir-up proposal, Cod 678," the Talkeroon observed. "It will require a lot of talkation before we decide to accept such a stir-up proposal."

"It certainly will," the President agreed. "But I think the First Look's suggestion should be put before Talkery, though of course I express no opinion about its yesness or noness."

"I shall certainly support its yesness," said Bum 444, receiving a cordial smile from the First Look in acknowledgment. "I have not forgotten what Bosworth One told me about useless mugs being allowed to remain in Boojumania."

"Well, well, we mustn't start the talkation until it is put before Talkery," the other two Pinks were reminded by Jaz 119.

"The Talkeroon is right," said the President, leading the way to the escalator from the peepery to the self-walk back to the Pink House.

When we arrived, the three Pinks made their farewells, but not before inviting Tin Pan and me to visit them.

"You shall attend a talkation," said Jaz 119.

"You shall see how difficult it would be for a fizzer to unload any Boojums on Lunamania unknown to the Lookalty," said Cod 678.

"And I am hoping to show you what our gimpers can do and how hard they work to do it," said Bum 444.

Tin Pan and I followed the President into the Pink House, where he was informed that Tod 51 was with his mother in the bowery.

"Ah, I am glad to learn that my mother is taking such an interest in you," said the President. "Tod 51 is a very lucky young mug because my mother will always give him good advice. He is also lucky to have the opportunity to learn much about Boojumania which in the future may be of great advantage to his career in the Management."

With these words the President took us with him to the bowery, where we were greeted with cordiality by Sex 715.

"There you are again. Did you enjoy the feetball? I'm getting a little too old for it nowadays."

"It was a wonderful match," the President told his mother with enthusiasm.

"I am sure it was," she commented. "And I am very glad that First Town won because Lunatic City is rather inclined to think that it must always overdo everybody else."

"Bum 444 was very happy," said the President.

"Dear Bum 444," his mother murmured, "he deserves such a pleasure. Nobody has done more for Gimpery than he has."

"He asked if the people in First Town could be given vitalot 12 at Third Eat," the President said.

"He is right. And I hope Tod 51 will be able to offer our Boojum guests vitalot 12."

"Yes, I had already thought of that. You have made arrangements, Tod 51, for our guests?"

"I have made all arrangements, Dad 333."

"Bum 444 will give you gimper beds if you ask him."

"I have already put in an application at the Office of Gimpery."

"Good mug, good mug," the President beamed. Then he turned to us.

"Well, Bosworth One and Tin Pan One, I shall leave you in the care of Tod 51, who knows that it will be his duty to provide for your comfort and to make arrangements for you to see whatever we have to show you in the Everlasting Lunatic Republic."

Tod 51 looked through his legs at the President and made the conventional salutation of farewell with his clenched fists.

D*

I felt I must show my appreciation of the President's hospitality, courtesy and kindness by doing in Rome as Rome did. I turned my back, bent over and held my clenched fists out through my legs.

"Very good, very good," Sex 715 chuckled.

Tin Pan choked back his Celestial conservatism and followed my example. Unfortunately he slipped. It was for him a sad loss of face, or rather of behind.

## Chapter 7

ALTHOUGH he was getting on for seventy, Tod 51 still had the blue of youth on his cheeks, but so had Pup 301, who was ninety-five. I am now, after nearly a year's residence in the Lunatic Republic, sometimes able to distinguish one Lunatic from another, but for a long time after our arrival every Lunatic looked alike, and if I had said when I first met him that Tod 51 resembled Pup 301 I should have supposed I was uttering a truism. Now I realise that in fact Tod 51 and Pup 301 are a little more alike than most Lunatics, and I appreciate why I immediately took a fancy to Tod 51: he reminded me of Pup 301, for whom I still retain warm feelings of gratitude for the way we were received at the look-house when we first reached the Moon, and I am happy to say that our friendship is still as firm as ever. I have no doubt from the kindness Tin Pan and I have received since we have been guests of the Lunatic Republic that any other lookmug would have received us with equal good-will, but first impressions are the strongest, and Pup 301 and Tod 51 will always be remembered by me with affection. As I write these words I reflect that it is most unlikely I shall ever have to remember them because I shall probably be much in their company for the next hundred years.

"We must now arrange about your beddings and eatings," Tod 51 announced as the upstep took us to the self-walk. Escalators are called 'upsteps' and 'down-steps' in Lunatic. "I have found good cells for you in Hive 6."

I have mentioned the lack of privacy in the sanaton-covered buildings along the self-walk. We were told by

Tod 51 that these were the work centres and that the inhabitants of Lunatic City all lived in the great hives which went towering up to what I found later was a kind of synthetic sky. There were nine hundred and nine of these hives, each of them with nine hundred and ninety cells. Hive 6, where cells had been found for Tin Pan and myself, was close to Pinkhall.

"Hardly half an oop," said Tod 51. But as I have already said, Einstein himself would have been baffled to comprehend distance in terms of oops, and after nearly a year in the Lunatic Republic I am still unable to grasp the system of Lunatic measurement. Tin Pan insists that he understands it; I do not believe him.

"It was lucky for me that we were notified in the Home Management by the Office of Arrival and Departure that Kix 78 and Zog 486 left Lunamania at A-time."

"You work in the Home Management?" I asked.

"Yes, I am a chairmug, and I am very pleased that I have been chosen to give you a picture of the Lunatic Republic because that will take me for some time away from Pinkhall. I have a cell in Hive 7, and they will put in a you-to-me quickspeak so that you can communicate at once with me without having to use the public quick-speak."

"How many oops is Hive 7 from Hive 6?" asked Tin Pan, anxious to show his superior powers of calculation.

"Two or three. It is just the other side of the self-walk."

And that reply kept Tin Pan quiet while he tried to work out by mental arithmetic how Hive 6, which was half an oop from the Pink House, could be two or three oops away from Hive 7.

A few minutes later we stepped off the self-walk and took an upstep leading to a spacious terrace on which were several large groups of sculpture in karnikon. I had not the faintest idea what they were supposed to represent, but then I have not the faintest idea what most groups of sculpture on Earth represent to-day.

"I am so pleased that we could find you cells in Hive 6, because this terrace is famous all over the Lunatic Republic for the work of our great sculptor Muk 13."

I looked at the groups, which slightly resembled a number of large pink eels with holes through them, but I was not prepared to commit myself and asked Tod 51 what the theme was. I thought this was probably a safer question than a suggestion that they might be intended to represent something."

"They are the essence of nuclearity," he replied.

"I see," I murmured, trying to look as wise as the art critic of a Sunday newspaper. "The essence of nuclearity, eh? Wonderful."

To myself I was wondering how anybody could extract useful and practical thinking out of this concatenation of perforated pink eels, and I was glad when we reached the entrance of Hive 6 without my being called upon to attempt to comment further upon the work of Muk 13, for I did not speak artistic jargon with any fluency.

The ground floor of Hive 6 at G-time was filled with hivers sitting about and gabbling to one another on rocking-chairs about the great feetball match.

When we entered with Tod 51, all the mugs and wugs rose from their chairs and greeted us with the gesture of welcome, to which I made the conventional gesture of hurrying into the circle.

Tod 51 produced from his pocket a microphone, which the Lunatics call a tongue-pot, and from the crimson and carmine walls of the Hive 6 chatterbox his voice could be heard from big-speaks all round the great room.

"Mugs and wugs of Hive 6 of Lunatic City, it is my joy to tell you that the two Boojums who arrived from Boojumania last night have been awarded by Home Management the cells of Kix 78 and Zog 486 who left Lunamania during the night. They have been received by our beloved President, Dad 333, and have had the treat of watching the feetball match from his peepery. The President announces that by an Action of Talkery this morning Bosworth One and Tin Pan One have been granted the hospitality of the Everlasting Lunatic Republic. You in Hive 6 will have the treat of friendly chatter and dancing and eating with our two Boojum friends."

When Tod 51 made this announcement, all the mugs and wugs in the great chatterbox jumped about and clapped their hands.

"They are very glad," said Tod 51, turning to Tin Pan and myself. "Will you notify to them that you are very glad?"

I realised that we were expected to show our pleasure by similar gestures and I at once began to jump about and clap my hands. Tin Pan did a lot of bowing; I knew that this was not enough.

"You must jump about, Mr Tin Pan," I said. "We must not offend our hosts."

Tin Pan had the sense to do as I urged, and I must admit that his performance did not lack dignity in spite of the pained expression upon his face.

"Bosworth One and Tin Pan One wish me to thank you, mugs and wugs of Hive 6, for the cordial welcome you have given them. And now please go on with your chatter because I must show our guests to their cells."

As we passed from the chatterbox to the upstep, the

noise of the conversation was twice as loud as when we came in. Evidently our arrival had been a great excitement for Hive 6.

We stepped off at the eatery on the floor above. It was spacious and circular, of the bright magenta hue we had seen in the President's Eat Room. There must have been about fifty large round tables, surrounded by low circular benches with accommodation for twenty eaters.

"I am arranging for you to have your two seats raised and also for a special tray. They will be ready at I-time for Third Eat. I shall take Third Eat with you because I want to be sure that you do not feel unusual. And now we shall go to your cells. You are cell 562, Bosworth One," he continued, leading the way to the upstep, "and Tin Pan One is cell 820."

However, we did not ascend immediately to our cells, but left the upstep two floors higher to visit the sittery, the cookery being above the eatery.

"The hivers will come at H-time to look at the great feetball match on the see-all before they step down to the eatery at I-time."

The sittery was another large hall in which the hivers sat on tiers of low benches to look at the see-all screen which occupied the whole of the far side of it.

I asked Tod 51 what the programme was for this evening. The word puzzled him, but I was able to explain what I meant.

"Everybody will look at the great feetball match which they saw at F-time and which they are now chattering about."

Above the sittery was the dansery, but we continued up to the fifth floor and walked along a wide corridor to cell 562, by the size of which I was agreeably surprised. The use of the word cell had prepared me for something much smaller.

"That is good," said Tod 51. "Your bed is already come from the Management of Gimpery. Lie down, please."

I tried my length on the bed, which had a comfortable air-mattress and allowed me plenty of room to stretch my legs.

"To-morrow," Tod 51 announced, "a clothmug will come to make you both two dresses. The Karetaker of the Kurarium has asked for your Boojum dresses to be handed over for preservation and public exhibition. And now please try these two gimper chairs."

"They are not very comfortable," I commented when Tin Pan and I were seated in two chairs with high straight backs and extremely hard seats. Tod 51 shook his head.

"No, I was afraid you might not find them comfortable. But to-morrow you will have rocking-chairs of gimper size. The gimpers themselves are not allowed to have rocking-chairs because with so much activation all day it is considered better for them to sit absolutely still until K-time, when they go to sleep."

"Certainly nobody would feel inclined to rock about in a chair like this," I agreed. "However, if I could have a higher table I could use one of these chairs when I want to do my writing."

"But you will never rite in the hive," Tod 51 assured us. "No riting is done anywhere in the Lunatic Republic except in the Omnibum. We shall go there to-morrow or perhaps the next day and I shall ask the knowall management if they will allocate a ritery to Tin Pan One and yourself at D-time."

I have spelt 'ritery' without a preliminary 'w' in Lunatic style.

"That is when the Lunatics work?"

"Yes, after First Eat until Second Eat at E-time," Tod 51 told us.

In the corner of my spacious cell stood what looked like a large metal bottle from which the neck had been knocked off, leaving a hole at the top rather wider than a head. I asked Tod 51 what this piece of furniture was for.

"That is one of the new brushabouts."

"Brushabout?" I repeated in perplexity. Tod 51 opened the front of the brushabout and I saw that the inside was not unlike the outside of a porcupine. Then he pressed a button and all the quills went into a state of what seemed frenzied movement.

"It was invented by one of our most respected know-alls, Nib 234, and it was considered such a valuable contribution to the welfare of lunamanity that he was awarded by Talkery, the highest decoration of the Lunatic Republic, the nine-point Pink Star. Until Nib 234 perfected his brushabout too much time was wasted by mugs and wugs in brushing one another at A-time and K-time."

"As the lookmugs still do," I commented.

"Yes, but it will not be very long now before all the look-houses are equipped with brushabouts. As soon as every hive in Lunatic City and the Lunatic Towns have their brushabouts, the look-houses will have theirs. It is lucky that after many months of talkation Talkery voted at last for gimpers to be given brushabouts. At first it was feared that the abolition of brushing one another might injure teaminess. However, the argument that gimpers should be spared any unnecessary activation at last prevailed. It is lucky, I say, because I do not know how you and Tin Pan One would have put yourselves inside the ordinary brushabout. It would have been difficult at A-time and K-time for you to take the upstep to brush Tin Pan One or for Tin Pan One to take the downstep to brush you."

I asked Tod 51 if it would be possible for us to have looking-glasses in our cells.

"Looking-glasses?" he echoed in astonishment. "Why do you want looking-glasses? You cannot see Booju-mania from Lunatic City."

I suddenly recalled that looking-glass was the word used by Pup 301 for a telescope and tried to explain to Tod 51 what I meant by a looking-glass. It was useless.

"To see yourself," he exclaimed. "But why do you want to see yourself? If you look at Tin Pan One you can see yourself, and if Tin Pan One looks at you he can see himself. You have more nails, yes, but that is all the difference."

I glanced at my finger-nails and then remembered that 'nail' was the Lunatic equivalent of 'inch'. He merely meant I was taller than Tin Pan. I was a little disconcerted for a moment by the realisation that my face must be as bright a blue as Tin Pan's, but more disconcerted to realise that like all Europeans who spend much time in China I had already begun to look Chinese.

"Well, I shall want to see myself for shaving."

"Shaving?" Tod 51 almost gasped. "Is that the way Boojums clean themselves? With a shave-box?"

I thought at first he meant a safety-razor, but soon it transpired that in Lunatic a shave-box was the equivalent of a carpenter's plane with which the shavemugs smoothed the various materials they were called to work upon. No doubt they were fearsome instruments, and it is not surprising that Tod 51 was puzzled.

"But why do Boojums shave their faces?" he asked.

"To remove the growing hair."

"Hair on the face!" he exclaimed. "Boojums have hair on their faces? That is the most dirty thing I have ever heard."

"The doormugs at the Pink House had hair."

"Gimpers grow jawmould when they become trainers," Tod 51 said.

"Do they consider it a dirty habit?"

"No," he admitted a little grudgingly. "But gimpers are gimpers."

I was on the point of asking Tod 51 why hair on the chin should be considered dirtier than the hair of eyebrows or eyelashes when I realised that he himself had neither. I looked at Tin Pan and saw that his slanting eyebrows had vanished. I put a finger quickly up to my forehead and found that my own had vanished likewise. The reader may well ask why I had not realised before now that Lunatics had neither eyebrows nor eyelashes; he must be indulgent to a human being a quarter of a million miles away who has just passed through an experience such as no human being has ever been called upon to pass through before.

I decided to change the subject of hair on the face and suggested that we might now take the upstep to Cell 820, where Tin Pan was to be accommodated.

Tin Pan's cell was exactly like mine, with the same metallic blue walls and ceiling and floor. I say 'metallic', for that was the effect, but on closer examination the material was evidently some kind of plastic. I asked Tod 51 what it was called.

"Kompo 1," he replied. "All cells in the hives of the Republic are the same. There was a talkation in Talkery some years ago because First Lunatic Town wanted to use Kompo 2 for their cells." He chuckled. "First Lunatic Town is always a little wanting to be Lunatic City, and Talkery knows that. So they were not allowed to use Kompo 2. Pinkhall was against it, and the First Town M.T.s who advocated Kompo 2 were outvoted. I hope their win this afternoon will not be putting ideas into their brainpots," he went on. "You must have noticed how puffish they were about their success. That's what they were all chattering about in the chatterbox. I shall not be at all surprised if the First Town M.T.s start a talkation after this puffery of theirs over winning the match at F-time."

At this point Tin Pan, who had been examining his cell, asked what was the meaning of a lavender-coloured ear with a crimson button beside it on the wall.

"That is your quickspeak," Tod 51 told him," when you want to speak to me in Hive 7."

Soon after this a noise between a whistle and a hoot sounded along the corridor, we were told that this was the signal for all the hivers to go up to the sittery and watch the see-all, and the three of us walked along to the downstep. I knew that we were going to see the feet-ball match we had seen at F-time, but I had supposed this was because it had been such an important and exciting match. However, I was soon to learn that whatever sport had been seen at F-time, provided that some special ceremony like the formal swearing in of a new President had not been taking place, was always shown again at H-time.

"You never have plays?" I asked Tod 51.

"Yes, we always have whatever play we had seen at F-time."

"I meant theatrical plays."

Tod 51 had evidently never heard of theatrical plays, and I tried to explain to him about the drama on Earth.

"You mean that in Boojumania you sit and watch

something that never happened!" he exclaimed. "That is a strange way to behave. Will you tell the knowalls in the Omnibum about—what is it you call it?"

"The drama."

"About the drama," Tod 51 repeated. "They will find it hard to believe that Boojums can be so senseless. Do you and Tin Pan One ever watch this drama?"

"Yes, yes," Tin Pan replied, "though of course we consider our Chinese drama much superior to the drama elsewhere."

"But how can one something about nothing be better than another something about nothing? They must all be equally silly."

At that moment we reached the entrance of the sittery, and rather to my relief Tod 51 did not continue to question us about the drama.

While I was watching the progress of the feetball-match I was reflecting to myself that with the ever-growing devotion to sport on earth the time might not be so far away when humanity would be as much pre-occupied with sport as lunamanity. When colour became general on television, there had been a revival of the drama, but in recent years the amount of time allotted to dramatic advertisement has been making the viewing public demand more and more sport when it was not looking at advertisements or listening to politicians giving evasive answers to interviewers at airports.

Suddenly all the mugs and wugs in the sittery stood up and began to clap their hands and jump about.

"They are seeing you now with the President," Tod 51 said.

Yes, my face was indeed an even brighter blue than Tin Pan's. Perhaps it would be better for me if I never did get back to Earth. Blue might be an insuperable colour bar wherever I landed.

As soon as the match was over on the screen, we all went down to the eatery. By this time I was feeling hungry and I helped myself generously from the big bowl of bixifit when it arrived from the cookery by way of the roof, like the plates at the Pink House. After we had eaten our bixifit, the empty plates were put into the empty bowl which was then taken up to the apertures in the roof. After this, plates of lavender-coloured vitalots descended and each one was passed round by means of a revolving disc in the centre of the table. The senior mug or wug at each table then held up a hand and said 'one, two, three, chew', after which all chewed away at the vitalots as they had done at the look-house until at each of the tables somebody held up a hand and called 'chew-hoo' three times to proclaim that he or she had been the first to consume the vitalot and so would be entitled to have two vitalots at Third Eat next day.

Although I had enjoyed the tasteless bixifit, I had not yet discovered the pleasure of chewing the equally tasteless vitalot, and I asked Tod 51 what it was that made the Lunatics so eager to win this contest.

"You feel twice yourself when you have two vitalots," he told me.

"In that case, why isn't everybody allowed two?" I asked.

"Because if everybody felt twice himself all the time it might lead to trouble, but when a mug feels twice himself perhaps only once in a year no harm is done."

When Third Eat was over, we all took the upstep to the dansery, where for a couple of hours or more to the sound of a huge mechanical organ the hivers indulged in a dance which resembled the rock 'n' roll that was so popular for a few years on earth, until people tired of it about thirty years ago. Occasionally the monotony of the dancing was varied by some of the younger mugs dancing upside down on their hands.

Tod 51 urged Tin Pan and myself to dance with two wugs to whom he offered to introduce us, but neither of us felt that he would do credit to humanity by his performance and both of us pleaded unfamiliarity with the dance to excuse ourselves. I should add here that after a year's residence in the Lunatic Republic both Tin Pan and myself dance every evening at J-time after Third Eat, though neither of us has yet attempted to dance upon his hands instead of his feet. However, on this first evening Tin Pan and I were both feeling rather tired and I asked Tod 51 if we might retire to our cells before the dancing stopped.

"But it is not K-time yet," he protested, obviously embarrassed by my suggestion: "nobody goes to his cell before K-time."

"The hivers would think it strange if Tin Pan One and I left the dansery early?" I asked.

"They would think it unusual. We puff ourselves in the Lunatic Republic upon everybody doing the same thing at the same moment. Indeed, we consider it our greatest achievement since we managed to survive the Abominable War."

"We wouldn't like to do anything that might upset people," I assured our guide.

"I think I can explain so that they will not think it unusual," said Tod 51. With this he took a tongue-pot from his pocket and presently his voice was heard above the organ from the bigspeaks round the dansery.

"Mugs and wugs of Hive 6," he began, and the dancers stopped to listen, "our Boojum friends are feeling tired after their long journey from Boojumania." There was a murmur of sympathetic comprehension from the hivers. "And so I hope you will understand why I shall take them up to their cells before K-time. I am anxious to do this so that I may be able to return to Hive 7 before K-time myself."

Loud clapping by the assembled hivers signified their approval of Tod 51's proposal, and we followed him out from the dansery to the upstep.

I have been postponing any mention of day and night in the Lunatic Republic because it is impossible for me to attempt any explanation of it. I can merely record that, whether the sun is shining for a fortnight or whether it is starlight for a fortnight it is always dark from K-time to A-time and light from A-time to K-time. How this is managed I have no idea. Tin Pan has gone into the question and has tried several times to expound his theories to me, but I do not even understand how a telephone works on earth, and television remains for me a perpetual miracle. So I remain in a state of happy ignorance.

It may be remembered that I was struck by the luminous heads of hair which the lookmugs extinguished by combing and I wondered whether my hair would become luminous as quickly as my body had turned blue. I had not noticed any luminous heads of hair among the hivers in the dansery and I asked Tod 51 about this, to be told that only the lookmugs had luminous hair.

"They sometimes have to bump about the Great Lunarian Waste when one of your Boojum fizzers is reported to have landed, and it is useful when they have to explore deep hollows which the light of Boojumania does not reach. Otherwise they might lose one another. Do not worry, Bosworth One, your hair is the same as it was when you arrived in Lunatic City this morning. And now I will say 'beddo' and take Tin Pan One to his cell. When the woo-hoo sounds for First Eat, you will know which is your table."

I presumed that 'woo-hoo' must be the name for that sound between a hoot and a whistle which announced the various times.

"Will the woo-hoo sound at A-time?" I asked.

"No, it will be A-time when you wake."

"But suppose I don't wake?"

"Everybody wakes at A-time," Tod 51 said.

"But in Boojumania we sometimes oversleep."

"Oversleep? What is that?" he asked.

I tried to explain, but evidently the notion of sleeping longer than anybody else was beyond his comprehension.

"Boojumania must be indeed a very strange place," he commented, "if some Boojums sleep longer than other Boojums. You must always be in a terrible muddle about time. I shall come at D-time with the clothmug, and if you want to ask me anything when I am not with you, press the button of the quickspeak. And now, Tin Pan One, I will take you to your cell."

As he and Tin Pan went out, Tod 51 turned, and putting a hand over each eye said, "Beddo, Bosworth One, beddo."

I realised that 'beddo' was the equivalent of our 'good-night' and putting a hand over each of my eyes I said "Beddo, Tod 51."

When I was alone, I stood for a while looking out at the amber light which suffused the hives of Lunatic City and pleasantly illuminated my cell. Then I undressed and saw that my body was as blue as that of an ancient Briton in his warpaint of woad.

"Now for the brushabout," I murmured to myself.

I opened the door and gazed nervously at the quills with which it was lined. I pressed the button; the quills did not move. Then I got inside and after closing the door pressed the button again. This time the quills moved with the noise of an angry swarm of bees. I found too that I was standing on what felt like a living doormat. I tried to open the door of the brushabout and escape from it; I could not move it. For about a minute I felt as if . . . well, it is really impossible to describe the sensation, but when the quills were suddenly quiet I found I could open the door and get out. I looked at my body, convinced that it must be covered with scratches; there was not a mark anywhere and I was not even tingling. Instead I felt as much refreshed as if I had enjoyed a hot bath. But what about my teeth? Why had I not asked Tod 51 how the Lunatics cleaned their teeth? About ten minutes later the woo-hoo sounded for K-time and in the hope that Tod 51 would be back in his cell in Hive 7 I pressed the button of the quickspeak. To my relief his voice replied.

"It's about my teeth," I told him. "I can't find a toothbrush in my cell."

"A toothbrush?" he repeated in astonishment.

"Yes, I want to clean my teeth."

"But the Third Eat vitalot cleans our teeth," he told me. "Do Boojums clean their teeth with a brush? What long ago people you are in Boojumania!"

"I'm sorry to have disturbed you, Tod 51."

"Did you manage to work the brushabout properly?"

"Yes, it worked splendidly."

"Well, beddo again. I was just going to get into my brushabout when the quickspeak rang."

The quickspeak was silent and I decided to get into bed as I was, because the bedclothes were so soft and silky and the temperature of my cell was so equable. Five minutes later the amber light turned to a deep blue and I immediately fell fast asleep.

## Chapter 8

TIN PAN knocked at the door of my cell at B-time next morning so that we could go down together to First Eat. I asked him how he had slept.

"Without a dream," he replied. "I have not slept so well for many years."

"The process of egalitarian achievement must always be worrying until it is complete," I observed. "But here in the Lunatic Republic where it was achieved centuries ago there seems nothing to worry about and so sleep is dreamless. How did you get on with the brushabout?"

"I was a little afraid at first," Tin Pan admitted, "because I was asking myself if the mechanism had gone wrong and, if it had, how I should avoid being brushed away altogether. I think our skins must have been toughened when they turned blue; otherwise we would certainly have been covered with scratches. Do you find our earthly clothes a little too warm to be pleasant?"

"I do, but Tod 51 will be here at D-time with the clothmug and I have no doubt that the Lunatic attire will be more suitable to the climate."

"I doubt whether you are correct in alluding to the climate, Mr Bosworth. A climate depends on natural atmospheric conditions, whereas here there do not appear to be any natural atmospheric conditions. As you may have heard, the Celestial Academy of Science is hopeful of readjusting climatic conditions all over the world in order to provide an equable climate everywhere, but it would be rash to claim that they have any immediate prospect of success. I hope to study the methods by which the Lunatics have overcome greater difficulties through lack of atmosphere, and if I should ever be successful in returning to earth I may be able to provide even the Celestial Academy of Science with facts of which it was ignorant."

Tin Pan corrected himself quickly for what might seem to imply a criticism of the Academy. . . . "With facts which it had not yet fully considered. For instance . . ."

But I did not pay attention to Tin Pan's theories, which I lacked the scientific training to appreciate . . . or even to understand. Moreover, I was feeling ready for the bixifit of First Eat, and when the woo-hoo sounded I jumped up eagerly to join the throng of hivers moving in the direction of the downstep.

After First Eat we returned to my cell to wait for Tod 51 and looked down at D-time to watch the hivers streaming out towards the self-walk which would take them to wherever their work lay.

A few minutes later Tod 51 arrived with Tak 365, the clothmug. The reader may wonder how I am able to remember all these names and numbers; I should not have been able to do so unless I had entered them in a small notebook which the Chinese authorities had luckily not confiscated when I was put in Heavenly Dragon.

Tak 365 lost no time in measuring Tin Pan and myself for our Lunatic attire, and by the time the woo-hoo sounded for Second Eat we were both equipped with a pair of blue Tweedledum and Tweedledee breeches which buttoned round a blue shirt with a broad open collar. Unlike the dress of the wugs, our shoes were part of the breeches. The material rather resembled nylon in appearance, but it did not have the slithery effect of nylon and it felt like genuine silk and wool. Underclothing was not worn in the Lunatic Republic, and I am bound to say I was pleased to be rid of the vest and underpants which I had been finding increasingly superfluous.

Tod 51 told us that there had been some discussion about our wearing blue or pink. One or two of the chair-mugs at Home Management had argued that as guests of the Lunatic Republic we were in a way official and should therefore be dressed in pink, but it was finally decided that we should wear the blue worn by the great majority of the hivers.

It was about a quarter of an hour before the woo-hoo sounded at E-time, that Tak 365 brought us our suits, and when we presented ourselves in the eatery all the hivers stood up and clapped.

"They are very pleased," said Tod 51, "because you now look like all other Lunatics. It is a terrible thing for a Lunatic to feel he looks different from others."

"But does any Lunatic ever look different from others?" I asked.

"It has happened," said Tod 51. "Only ten years ago a wug was given a pink mugling and she was so much upset that she wouldn't chew her vitalots and left Lunamania when she was only thirty years old."

"What happened to the mugling?"

"The knowalls did their best to turn him blue, but they did not succeed. So after a talkation in Talkery it was decided that the kindest thing to do was to let the pink mugling leave Lunamania too because his life would be so sad as an unusual."

After Second Eat we went with Tod 51 at F-time to the gimpasium to see what the Lunatics call a kikwikery match between the gimpers of Lunatic City and Fifth Lunatic Town. Kikwikery is the nearest sport to boxing that the Lunatics have, but instead of hitting each other with their fists in gloves they put their feet in gloves and fight upside down. Besides the kikwikery there were wrestling matches in the catch-as-catch-can style. Wrestling is called squeezery, and the contest is won by the squeezer whose breath lasts longest. After the kikwikery and the squeezery there were running races both forwards and backwards. I found the backward races very exciting and marvelled at the speed attained by the runners.

Next day Tod 51 took us to the Great Kurarium, a most impressive edifice built of the pink stone called karnikon, which would have roused the envy of the most advanced earthly architect. If you can imagine a larger pyramid than the great pyramid of Egypt, on top of which is an equally large pink pyramid upside down, you will have some idea of the Kurarium. The pointed parts of the pyramids do not meet but are separated by an immense circular column of what looks like crystal. There are no windows in the Kurarium, and the interior is artificially lighted. Upsteps take the visitor through a series of rooms gradually diminishing in size until he reaches the column, which he ascends by a spiral upstep and so on up to the top of the Kurarium through a series of rooms gradually increasing in size.

In the ground floor hall we found three rockets and two sputniks on exhibition, at the sight of which Tin Pan seemed on the verge of jumping about and clapping his hands in Lunatic fashion.

"That is the Chinese rocket launched from the Gobi Desert in 1992 in the same year that the American rocket called Columbus the Second fell into the Caribbean Sea. You remember, Mr Bosworth, it was intended to celebrate the quincentenary of the discovery of America by sending two Americans to the Moon. What a joy it would be for the Celestial Academy of Science if they could know that their rocket had done what the Americans failed to do."

"But no Chinese went up in it," I reminded Tin Pan. He shook his head proudly.

"I am the first Chinese to reach the Moon."

"And they'll know no more about it in China than they know about the rocket they launched in 1992," I murmured gently. "Whose are the other two rockets?"

He shrugged his shoulders.

"They may be American or Russian or perhaps German," he replied.

"And these sputniks?"

"They are not Chinese," Tin Pan declared positively.

I asked Tod 51 if there was a printed catalogue of the objects shown in the Kurarium.

"No, because only knowalls and chairmugs are able to read words of more than one syllable, and all the other hivers would feel that knowalls and chairmugs were being given privilege. Privilege is the word that is the most hated word of all in the Lunatic Republic. Did you notice that when I said it just now I made a scrapeback with my feet?"

I had indeed noticed what he called the scrapeback, which had reminded me of a dog's defiant scrape with its hindlegs on saying good-bye to a lamp-post.

"Then most of the Lunatics do not know what any of these objects are," I commented.

Tod 51 smiled.

"The tell-speak will give them the gen."

"The gen?" I exclaimed, for you can imagine how surprised I was to find that piece of airforce slang an established word in the Lunatic Republic. Tod 51 went to a thin rod beside the rockets with what looked like a miniature trumpet on top, with a single stop. This he pressed and a voice came out of the trumpet.

"This Boojum fizzer came down on the edge of the Great Lunarian Waste in the year 3008 after the Abominable War and was the first fizzer the Lookalty was able to bring to the Kurarium of the Everlasting

Lunatic Republic. You will note the primitive work-manship indicating the low standard of lunatisation reached in Boojumania."

"That is certainly an American rocket," Tin Pan affirmed.

"Tin Pan One," Tod 51 protested, "rocket is a rude word in Lunatic."

"I excuse myself," said Tin Pan. "This is certainly an American fizzer. Can we now hear what is said about this fizzer?" He pointed to the one he had claimed for China.

Tod 51 pressed the stop on the next trumpet.

"This Boojum fizzer came down on the edge of the Great Lunarian Waste in the year 3041 after the Abominable War. It shows a very slight advance on the fizzers previously secured, but it is obviously the work of beings many thousands of years behind the Ever-lasting Lunatic Republic."

I made a sign to Tin Pan not to argue about this, and we passed on to the rod beside one of the sputniks.

"This appears to be an attempt to transport a Boojum from Boojumania to Lunamania in a round-about, but for gen about the unusual creature found inside, visitors to the Kurarium must take the upstep to Room 8 where the creature may be seen."

"After we have seen this creature," said Tod 51, "I will present you to Gup 99 the Karetaker, and you will be able to tell him whether this creature really is a Boojum mugling. They have been disputing about it in the Omnibum ever since it came to Lunamania six years ago."

"That was when the Russians sent up a monkey in a sputnik in 1991 in order to annoy the Americans."

And Tin Pan was right. When we reached Room 8 in the apex of the lower pyramid there on a stand was a small monkey which, considering that the Lunatics had never seen men or monkeys alive had been stuffed with creditable realism.

The tell-speak announced:

"This unusual creature was found inside the round-about shown in Room 1. It was believed at first to be a fully grown Boojum, but some of our knowmost knowalls argue that so small a creature could not have constructed even the clumsily designed fizzers which have reached Lunamania. It is now generally accepted that this is a very young Boojum, perhaps not yet a month old, which was placed in the roundabout in the hope that it would return to Boojumania alive after going round Lunamania; in which case the journey might be attempted by fully grown Boojums."

"This is what we call a monkey," I told Tod 51. "It is an animal: it is not a human being."

Tod 51 decided it was time to meet the Karetaker, or as we should say the Curator, of the Kurarium, and we took a spiral upstep through the column and went on until we reached the spacious top of the inverted pyramid where we were presented to Gup 99.

"And so it is not a Boojum," said the Karetaker after I had explained to him what the animal in the sputnik was. "Yet there is a certain likeness to you and Tin Pan One in this creature."

I might have answered that there was just as much likeness to him or Tod 51, but I refrained and tried to give him some notion of the animal world on Earth and, rather lamely I am afraid, to expound the theory of evolution.

Gup 99 shook his head.

"I find what you say incomprehensible."

"It is difficult to make the unknown comprehensible," I told him. "If in the future I should ever be in a

E

position to try to convey to my fellow-Boojums what life is like in the Lunatic Republic, they might find my account of it equally incomprehensible."

"Yet you and Tin Pan One do not seem so different from us. I know that our beloved President Dad 333, has been much impressed to find how lunatised you both are. What did you say you called this unusual creature we found in the roundabout?"

"A monkey, but that is what it is called in English. There are numerous other names for it in different parts of Boojumania."

"The English Boojums are evidently the most lunatised people in Boojumania," the Karetaker declared, "because we can understand what you speak and you can understand what we speak."

I considered for a moment whether I should try to explain to Gup 99 that the people who spoke English were not necessarily English, but I kept silent. I felt that 240,000 miles from the Earth I was safe from the protests of those who, while speaking English, regard it as an insult to be called English instead of British.

"We must correct the tell-speak," said Gup 99. "I have an idea, Bosworth One. You shall record with a tongue-pot what a monkey is. We have been telling people that it is a Boojum mugling when it is really a monkeyling."

"I think it is a fully grown monkey. There are various kinds of monkeys, and this is a small kind. Some monkeys are bigger than Lunatics."

"And they are able to make these fizzers?" Gup 99 asked.

"No, no," I replied hastily. "We regard the ability to make fizzers as something far beyond the intelligence of animals. The monkey is an animal."

And before I knew it I was once more plunged into

an attempt to explain the difference between men and animals. I invite my still unimaginable readers to try to describe even so familar an animal as a dog to a being who has never seen anything alive on four legs. If only the Russians had sent up another dog instead of a monkey I might have been able from that to give Gup 99 an idea of what tigers or deer or even warthogs looked like; but after the monument in Paris was raised forty years ago to Little Lemon as a martyr to Science the Russians were chary about upsetting Western feelings by sending up any more dogs, and monkeys were used instead. This was still resented by the more passionate animal-lovers, and many will remember the great libel action brought against the B.B.C. by Lord Northbrook when one of these animal-lovers suggested in a Brains Trust discussion that the noble lord or the editor of the *Daily Female* should be sent up in a satellite instead of a defenceless monkey.

"You say these dogs run on four legs," Gup 99 asked, "and that in Boojumania there are thousands of other animals, as you call them, who also move about on four legs? It is unbelievable."

"I have a friend who is Dog 268," said Tod 51. "He will laugh much when I tell him about these dogs in Boojumania."

"Is there an animal called Gup?" the Karetaker asked.

I assured him there was no such animal as a gup, but I was tactful enough not to tell him what gup did mean.

"Do you have bugaboos in Boojumania?" was the next question.

We had already heard of these monsters, and when Gup 99 described one to us Tin Pan immediately said they sounded like the mythical dragons of his native land.

"We have an attempted reconstruction of a bugaboo made from some bones and teeth discovered in the Great Lunarian Waste. You would like to see it, would you not? It is in the room underneath."

I must say I was not surprised that the pre-war Lunarians and Lunatians were driven to invent zoomers in order to exterminate such monsters.

"We cannot be perfectly sure that this is an exact reproduction of a bugaboo," Gup 99 told us when we stood before the huge shape, which measured at least a hundred feet from the tip of its scaly tale. This had a horny kind of rudder at the end of it, and scaly wings stretched out at least fifty feet on either side. The great open jaws were furnished with pointed teeth nearly a foot long.

"It is believed that the bugaboo was only vulnerable from above," said the Karetaker. "We have no reliable gen about the size of its wings, but we have assumed that they must have been as large as this attempted reconstruction of them; otherwise they would not have been able to sustain such a weight in the air. Unfortunately, beyond knowing that a hunting bugaboo could snap up more than twenty mugs in one swoop, we have no reliable gen about their habits. The accepted theory is that they roosted at the edge of precipices in the highest mountains. Their breeding habits remain a mystery, but we do know that they laid eggs."

"We use the word bugaboo in English for an imaginary terror," I said.

"I can assure you, Bosworth One, that the bugaboos of Lunamania were not at all imaginary," said Gup 99.

"No, indeed, but I was wondering whether we ever had bugaboos in Boojumania which were once upon a time a far from imaginary terror. You have no birds in Lunamania?"

"Birds? You still have birds?"

I tried to describe our birds, and had no success until I came to the ostrich.

"Ah," said Gup 99, "that sounds rather like a beekileg. After the Abominable War, when the Everlasting Lunatic Republic was struggling to survive, the Lunatics were driven to eat beekilegs. That is for us a most horrible thought, but we who to-day enjoy the result of what the Lunatics of three thousand years ago endured for us, honour the mugs and wugs of those days for the sacrifice they made. Once a year we keep Beekileg Day as a solemn eatnot. I will show you now a beekileg which was found in a perfect state of preservation by some karnikon miners. It is believed that it may have been deliberately hidden by an unlunatised Lunatic to provide himself with food in defiance of the basic rule upon which the Everlasting Lunatic Republic is founded—all for all. We do not like to think that there was ever a Lunatic capable of hiding food from his fellow-Lunatics, but there is no other plausible explanation of how this beekileg was found where it was found."

We went down to another room to look at the beekileg, and indeed it was very like an ostrich, though at least half as big again.

"It must have made very tough eating," I commented.

"Very tough," the Karetaker agreed. "They could not eat the legs. To this day in the bixifit growth sometimes the digmugs still find legs."

The beekileg in the Kurarium had no feathers, but was covered with fine hairs instead, and there was no sign even of an elementary wing.

"And now," said Gup 99, "I shall show you our newest exhibit. We have given it a very respectable place."

This respectable place turned out to be the room in the apex of the lower pyramid; there Tin Pan and I saw our earthly clothes displayed.

"And now will you please speak into the tongue-pot?" the Karetaker requested.

I suggested that Tin Pan should try to explain the mechanism of the protective covering in which we had been enveloped when we left the Gobi Desert, but this he was unwilling to do in case the Celestial Academy of Science should disapprove of its secrets being revealed.

"By the time any of your colleagues do what you have done, Mr Tin Pan, they will probably be everybody's secrets," I told him. However, Communist discipline was too strong for him even 240,000 miles away, and he excused himself by assuring the Karetaker of the Kurarium that none of the materials used could be found in Lunamania. So nothing was said about the protective covering and I faced the tongue-pot myself to explain what our ordinary attire was.

"This is what in Boojumania we call a suit of clothes, and it is the usual dress worn everywhere, varying in texture to suit the variations of heat and cold. What in the Lunatic Republic you call leggings and forks we call trousers and breeches. We have leggings in Boojumania, but they are made of leather, a tough animal substance . . ."

"Excuse me to poke in," said Gup 99, "but I do not think that Lunatic visitors to the Kurarium will be able to understand what animal means because these animals of which you have told us do not exist in Lunamania."

"Shall I just say tough substance without trying to explain what it is?"

"That will be very good."

"Made of a tough substance and only used to cover

the leg below the knee. It will be noticed that on each side of the upper part of the trousers are two openings. These are called pockets and are used to carry loose money."

"Money?" Gup 99 repeated. "What is that?"

"Money," I said, "is a metal token used for purposes of exchange for articles of food or clothing or indeed to buy anything offered for sale."

Gup 99 and Tod 51 were evidently mystified, and I was faced with the prospect of having to explain about money and buying and selling to people who if they ever have used money or bought or sold anything had certainly not done so for many centuries. I made an attempt and presently Gup 99 told me that the state of Boojumania seemed to be like the state of Lunamania when Lunaria and Lunatia were fighting one another about A the Mother of Life and O the Father of Life. At this time I had not read any of the Lunatic chronicles, and so I was as much mystified as the two Lunatics.

"I think I'd better leave out any reference to money when I explain about the pockets. Perhaps I'd better say nothing about pockets?"

"Oh yes, that will be interesting because what we call pockets are the sacks used by the bixifit gather-wugs."

"I'll say that the pockets of our trousers are some-times used to carry eats."

Gup 99 nodded approvingly, and I continued, "It will be noticed that the mugs in Boojumania wear boots or shoes separate from the trousers as wugs do in Luna-mania. The coverings used by Boojums for their feet are called socks."

At this point I asked if I might change the socks and shoes as they were arranged. I did not want Tin Pan's white cotton socks to be attributed to my shoes.

"It will be noticed that the Boojum trousers are buttoned vertically in front. These buttons are called fly-buttons."

"But why do they go up and down instead of round and round?" Gup 99 asked.

"It is a convenience for putting our trousers on and for something you do not have to do in the Lunatic Republic."

"Very clumsy," he commented. "Very clumsy indeed. Our leggings are much more lunatised. And you have buttons round and round as well. Why?"

"Those are for the braces which in parts of Boojumania are called suspenders. These pass over the shoulders and keep the trousers from falling down."

"I find that very clumsy too," Gup 99 observed.

"The sleeveless garment buttoning in front is called a waistcoat and allows the coat, or jacket as we also say, to remain open."

"Then why is it not called a chestcoat?" Gup 99 asked, pertinently I thought, for why is what is really a chestcoat called a waistcoat? I decided to evade the question by explaining the underclothing.

"The close-fitting garment covering the upper part of the body is worn next the skin for warmth and is called a vest. The word vest is also sometimes used for the waistcoat."

Gup 99 and Tod 51 shook their heads. The irrational behaviour of Boojums was beyond their comprehension.

"The garment worn next the skin of the lower part of the body is sometimes called a pair of drawers, but is more often alluded to as pants, though trousers are also called pants."

"But why, please, do you Boojums not know what is the name of something?" the Karetaker asked.

"Ah, that is the English way, because the English

have always been afraid of exactness," Tin Pan put in. "The Chinese are more exact."

I might have retorted that if we did have different words for the same thing we didn't have the same word for different things as in Chinese.

"We now come to the shirt," I continued, disdaining argument.

"We have shirts," exclaimed Gup 99, his tone a combination of satisfaction and relief. "But what is that thin piece of cloth?"

"That is a necktie."

"A necktie?" Gup 99 and Tod 51 simultaneously ejaculated. "Why must Boojums tie their necks? Do they break easily?"

I explained that neckties were worn more for display than for any practical purpose, and I tied my own grey silk tie under the wide collar of my blue Lunatic shirt, which was open at the neck and without buttons. Neither Gup 99 nor Tod 51 thought it added any attraction to ordinary Lunatic attire.

The next question that arose was who was the most suitable painter in the Lunatic Republic to preserve for the Kurarium the outward appearance of Tin Pan and myself dressed in our Boojum clothes. Apparently the habit of Lunatic artists to paint the inside of their subjects instead of their outside, because every Lunatic looked so much like the next, made it doubtful whether any of them would be able to make a satisfactory portrait of externals.

I asked if photography existed in the Lunatic Republic, but as far as I could make out it never had. No doubt the likeness that existed between all Lunatics had failed to inspire any inventor to discover a way of preserving the lineaments more easily than by portrait painting.

E*

"But does one of your Lunatic artists obtain recognition for a portrait of the inside let us say of your President? I mean, if his portrait was not labelled Dad 333, how could the average Lunatic know that it was intended to be Dad 333? How long have you been practising what we in Boojumania call abstract art, that is painting ideas rather than people or things?"

"For over five hundred years at least," the Karetaker assured us.

"We've not yet been going in for it in Boojumania for a hundred years, and many of us, indeed I could say most of us, have not the slightest notion yet what our advanced abstract painters are trying to portray."

"To be candid," Gup 99 admitted, "there are still quite a lot of people in the Lunatic Republic who even after five hundred years are still unable to recognise the originals of many of our portraits."

We were then asked if we should like to see the gallery of Lunatics who had deserved well enough of the Republic to have their portraits hung in the Kurarium.

I can only describe the effect of these portraits by saying that they made the wildest Picasso look like an old-fashioned Christmas card. There was one constant feature in all of them. The navel was always an eye in the middle of a small portion of blue stomach, and we were told to keep our gaze steadily fixed on this eye and to avoid trying to follow the convolutions all round it in detail; in that way we should obtain the impression that the painter was hoping to give.

"I'm afraid that however long I may be granted to live in Lunamania I shall never be able to appreciate or even to comprehend Lunatic art," I had to confess at last. "It occurs to me, too, that the most skilful of your Lunatic painters may have some difficulty in knowing what my inside or the inside of Tin Pan One is like."

"That is why I want to find a painter who can preserve your outsides," said Gup 99.

"There is a painter in Hive 7 who might have a try," Tod 51 suggested. "His name is Jaj 896. The other day he was showing me a picture he had made of the view from his cell and I could pick out the Pink House and the Office of Home Management without the slightest difficulty."

"Perhaps you will ask him to consult with me to-morrow?" Gup 99 suggested.

The sequel to this was that a few days later Tin Pan and I were invited to give sittings to Jaj 896. The only time I ever sat for a portrait was for me a tiresome experience, but sitting for Jaj 896 looked like proving an unpleasant ordeal because he insisted that we should pose for him upside down.

"But why?" I protested.

"Because you must have been upside down if you were shot up from Boojumania and came down in Lunamania."

"If we allow for the sake of argument that we were upside down when we landed on Lunamania we are not upside down now, and if you paint us upside down you will give an erroneous impression of what we look like," I maintained.

"Ah, but I want to preserve for the future your appearance when you reached Lunamania," said the painter obstinately.

I turned to Tod 51.

"You know Pup 301. He will tell you that when he first saw Tin Pan One and myself we were both the right way up."

It was no use. Jaj 896 was determined to paint us upside down and nothing that Tin Pan or I could say would induce him to change his mind. And then when

I was on the point of declaring that if I had to pose upside down I should refuse to pose at all, Tod 51 pointed out that Jaj 896's object could be attained by painting us the right way up and then hanging the pictures upside down. To our relief this solution of the problem was accepted by Jaj 896.

Some months later our insides were painted by Tit 32, who was considered the chief of all Lunatic painters. Mine looked like a plate of vermicelli being attacked by a pink haggis; Tin Pan's inside looked like a blue cow-pat.

## Chapter 9

IN the course of the next few days Tod 51 took us all over the high plateau of the Lunatic Republic, the extent of which so far as I could reckon seemed to be about four or five hundred square miles. It forms a very small portion of the Moon's surface, but is absolutely level, without an undulation anywhere on its surface until the foothills which lead to the ranges of mountains by which it is completely surrounded, except along the Great Lunarian Waste where Tin Pan and I landed from Heavenly Dragon. These mountains appear to be as tall as the giants of the Himalaya and the foothills are a desert of craters made during the Abominable War. In this desert are the various mines worked by the Lunatics.

Bearing in mind our journey from the time that Heavenly Dragon came down until we reached the outskirts of the Lunatic Republic, Tin Pan and I estimated that from the Earth it would be situated just over the other side of the Moon.

The Russians were claiming as far back as the early 'sixties to be sending sputniks round the moon, and the discovery of that sputnik with a small monkey inside proves that there was some justification for their claim. None of the sputniks has ever signalled back the phenomenon of an atmospheric area on the moon, but I suspect that the Chinese knew what they were trying to do when Tin Pan and I were shot up in Heavenly Dragon. In other words, I feel fairly sure they had guessed that there might be a habitable portion and had a notion whereabouts it was likely to exist. Moreover, I believe that Tin Pan was aware of this theory, though he refuses to admit to me that there was such a theory. I should not be at all surprised if in the near future another rocket with human beings inside came down near where we came down in Heavenly Dragon, but will the people inside enjoy the good luck that Tin Pan and I enjoyed?

What a foolish question! For nearly a year I have tried not to speculate about the future; if I begin to speculate I shall begin to fret, and existence here will become intolerable.

Lunatic City, except for the district of Pinkhall, is merely a larger edition of the nine Lunatic Towns, all of which are exactly alike and divided from one another by the same flat expanses of the bixifit plantations. Yet the sporting contests every day at F-time are able to provide enough civic rivalry to make the hiver in Lunatic First Town feel proud not to be a hiver in Lunatic Ninth Town, or vice versa. Moreover, all the Lunatic towns have a sane, good-natured provincial contempt for the metropolis, which of course is reciprocated. Nine days every year are devoted to an attempt by the gimpers of the Nine Towns in combination to become the champions of the Lunatic Republic at the expense of the gimpers of Lunatic City—to run faster, to kikwik and to squeeze harder, to bound higher and farther, and to score the winning points at feetball. When we visited Lunatic First Town we found the hivers were still discussing the match we had seen from the President's peepery and predicting confidently that when the annual Ninery came round Lunatic City would be deprived of the championship which it had now held for three years in succession. This in fact, to their great elation, the Nine Towns did succeed in doing.

The average Lunatic with whom I talked was most anxious to hear about sport in Boojumania, and even the knowalls and chairmugs, although they felt it was their duty to ask learned questions about life in Boojumania, almost always came back in the end to questions about sport.

All were fascinated by my account of horse-racing, and I understand that the experiment of mounting digmugs on gimpers in an attempt to provide the equivalent of horse-racing in the Lunatic Republic may presently be debated in Talkery.

Tod 51 took us to see the bixifit plantations, and as I watched the digmugs at work the impression of an antlike efficiency was strong. So it was in the karnikon mine at the edge of the crater-covered foothills leading up to the mountains. I asked Tod 51 how it was settled who should work in the mines, and was told that it was by drawing lots.

"But no mug works in the mines for more than a year, and in the following year he is always given one of the easy jobs in the bixifit growth," he added.

When we had been taken round some of the bixifit plantations I decided that growth was a more expressive word for its cultivation than plantation. The great belt-like fronds with pods filled with six-inch beans do not need to be trained to what I had thought were a kind of hop-poles when I saw them first from the self-walk on the way to Lunatic City with Pup 301. These magenta metallic poles are there for the gatherwugs to swarm up and cut the pods. Then the stripwugs below fill the sacks, or pockets as they are called, with the beans. The pods themselves are collected to be taken to 'weaveries' for the standard cloth. The beans and the empty pods are loaded on the huge self-wagons travelling back and forth between Lunatic City and the bixifit growth. In the nine Lunatic Towns the procedure is the same.

According to our earthly experts, as the population of mankind increases the human race will be dependent for survival on its ability to extract food from the sea, both in the shape of sea-weed and by some process by which plankton can be adapted to human consumption. I wonder if five centuries hence the diet of mankind will be as tasteless as that of the Lunatics. But will that matter, when by that time all mankind will have lost its sense of taste?

I asked how the bixifit was propagated and was told that nothing more was necessary than sticking a piece of the stalk into the ground. The main labour of the bixifit growth was turning the powdery soil, which had to be done constantly by the digmugs allotted to this task.

I have already mentioned that all the Lunatic buildings except the Pink House, the Kurarium, and the House of Talkery, whether residential hives or factories, are made of this glassy material called sanaton. I should have added that the framework and floors and inner walls are made of some plastic material called stikon, the weight of which is very light but the strength of which is extreme.

We were shown the great factory where stikon is produced, but I am ashamed to say I came out of it no wiser than I went in. Tin Pan professed to recognise all sorts of processes that the Chinese were beginning to develop, but my mind becomes a blank when people try to tell me how things are made in factories, and I should only confuse my technological readers and lose my untechnological readers if I attempted to explain.

We were also taken round some of the sanaton factories, where again I left bewildered by the process of turning air into something like glass. Another place which Tin Pan found of absorbing interest contains the gigantic pumps which supply the atmon that shelters the whole of the Lunatic Republic and becomes light or dark at will, regardless of the behaviour of the sun or the stars. The Earth, as my readers know, is never visible from the Lunatic Republic.

Tin Pan believed that the Chinese discovery of celestium might ultimately be developed to produce the lunar atmon, and he discoursed to me in a rhapsody of the time when the whole earth would be sheltered by celestium without wind, frost or snow, and with rain laid on as required.

"Then why is there no rain on the Moon?" I asked. "Why have the Lunatics had to substitute compression for moisture? Be careful you don't destroy all the vegetation on earth with your celestium experiments."

"We are still far away from such experiments," Tin Pan said. "We are only at the humble beginning of what Science is going to achieve. Oh, if I could only see what the earth will be like ten thousand years hence!"

I assured him fervidly that the thought of being exposed to such a prospect made me shudder and that my chief objection to Communism was the way it was leading mankind in the direction of such a prospect.

"It makes me sad when I hear you say such things, Mr Bosworth," Tin Pan sighed.

"It makes me much more sad when I think that never again will the world have a Homer or a Shakespeare or even a Burns or a Catullus to sing, that all your sublime Chinese art will belong to the past, and that man made in the likeness of God will turn to the likeness of a white or a red or a black ant. However, it is one consolation for remaining on the Moon for the rest of my life."

This brief exchange between Tin Pan and myself was not heard by Tod 51, who came along at that moment, I remember, to say that it was time we went to visit the Omnibum.

I had already learnt from Pup 301 that it was the luck of the draw which decided whether a mugling should leave school at twenty or continue to learn for another ten years and qualify at thirty either to enter the Omnibum or to become a chairmug in one of the Management Offices; once again the lot decided his future. I did not expect therefore to find any notable difference between the knowalls in the Omnibum and the great body of Lunatics. However, I was profoundly impressed by the Chief Knowall in the Omnibum who is called the Pantek, and it is significant that the Pantek is the only Lunatic who is elected to a responsible position instead of acquiring it by the luck of the draw; elected, moreover, by his fellow-knowalls and not by popular vote.

The Pantek's business is to direct the knowalls under him toward the tasks for which he considers them most suitable. The problem of life out of not-life has been for along time the object of the Omnibum's earnest solicitude, and towards this the Pantek directs his most promising young knowalls when they come to the Omnibum. Others are appointed to important research posts in the factories, but never to the administration of them, which is always a job for chairmugs. Others again keep records of events in the Lunatic Republic, and the records are always available for the various Management Offices in Pinkhall when the chairmugs wish to consult them.

Nob 9 had been Pantek now for over fifty years and he was held in such esteem as a repository of knowledge that perhaps only the unbroken rule of so many centuries, that a Lunatic should leave Lunamania on his hundred and ninety-ninth birthday, prevented a suggestion that Nob 9's stay on Lunamania should be extended; he was now a hundred and ninety-one years old.

I greeted with the deepest respect this venerable figure when I was presented to him by Tod 51. I say venerable figure, but, except for the paler blue of his ancient cheeks, there was no sign of age about him and he moved about the Great Omnibum as nimbly as the youngest knowall who had just arrived there from school.

"I am glad, very glad that I have been able to live long enough on Lunamania to see with my own eyes the first Boojums to visit the Everlasting Lunatic Republic. Our beloved President has spoken about you to me with affectionate regard for your lunatised behaviour. I have always believed myself that the fizzers which began to reach us nearly forty years ago were an indication of the curiosity of our nearest neighbours in space; I never thought that they had any hostile significance."

"They certainly had no hostile significance," I declared. "And they never will have any hostile significance. Curiosity is the only reason for sending out these fizzers."

"Scientific curiosity in the hope that we may add to our knowledge of conditions remote from the Earth," Tin Pan added primly.

"The Earth?" Nob 9 repeated.

"What you call Boojumania," I said quickly.

"You call it the Earth," Nob 9 went on. "We have a word in Lunatic for the time after the Abominable War when so many perished of starvation—the Dearth. There is no starvation on the Earth?"

"Not yet," I said. "But many of our knowalls fear that it may come because of the continuous increase of population."

The Pantek asked what the population of the Earth was, and when I told him he turned an even lighter blue.

"The population of the Earth is . . ." he stopped, evidently appalled by the immense figure. "But I do not think that the Earthatics—is that what you call yourselves?—will try to populate Lunamania. Your knowalls must be aware that almost the whole of it has been uninhabitable ever since the Abominable War."

"That is the opinion of our knowalls," I confirmed. "But it must be remembered that the other side of Lunamania is not visible from the Earth and therefore curiosity about that other side is inevitable."

"That is natural," said the Pantek.

"Both Tin Pan One and myself cannot help being puzzled that you in the Lunatic Republic, who in many ways are so much further advanced than we are on the Earth, have never made up your minds to visit us," I said.

"Yes, I can understand that," the Pantek agreed. "And I must admit that I did once try to persuade the Lunatic Management to undertake such an expedition. But it might have involved constructing large fizzers, and even now after three thousand years the horror of the Abominable War is still so much a present horror for us, the descendants of those who survived, that the idea of constructing any machines capable of rising above us is still too repugnant to be contemplated. So I think that Boojumania will never tempt the curiosity of the Everlasting Lunatic Republic. More recently, since these Boojum fizzers have been reaching us, there has been a movement in the Lookalty to build counter-fizzers in case we are attacked by Boojumania, but so far I have been successful in dissuading Talkery from authorizing such a step, and undoubtedly the great mass of the hivers are glad about this. But let us chatter about less disagreeable subjects. I have at least been granted the joy of meeting two Boojums and I warn you, Bosworth One, and you too, Tin Pan One, that I look forward to asking you both innumerable questions about that mysterious luminary which once upon a time many in Lunamania revered as the Mother of Life."

"We shall tell you all we know," I promised.

"You must both be patient with me," the Pantek said, "for there is so much I want to know and the time for learning grows short."

"Please ask us whatever you feel inclined to ask, Nob 9, though I must warn you that I am not technologically well equipped and may often disappoint you by my ignorance. Tin Pan One is a knowhow; I am not."

"It is not so much your knowhow achievement as your way of life that I want to hear about," Nob 9 assured me. "For instance, I am told by that remarkable wug Sex 715 that you have what seems to us a strange institution called marriage, which involves not only motherness but fatherness as well."

"That is so," I confirmed.

"The mother wug is called a wife?"

"Correct."

"And the father mug?"

"A husband."

"Ah, that must be what Sex 715 called the nonsense word she could not remember. You will understand that to us Lunatics the notion of such intimacy is unpleasant. I am using a mild word to express myself because I do not wish to offend two Boojums whom we are treating as welcome guests. But I think you will understand not merely how unpleasant such a relationship between mugs and wugs must seem to us, but also how utterly such a relationship must in our view upset the equality on which the Everlasting Lunatic Republic is based. There was a time when a part of Lunamania opposed the lunatised habit of artificial insemination, as we learn from the earliest chronicles that survive; but owing to the complete destruction of all Lunarian records in the Abominable War we know none of the arguments that the Lunarians used when the Lunatians first made artificial insemination obligatory. What we do know is that the Lunatic Republic would not have been everlasting if it had reverted to the primitive methods of survival that once upon a time had fervent advocates in Lunamania. We could not have controlled our population and so ensured comfort for all. We could not have prevented ambitious mugs from exploiting the muglings of whom they knew themselves to be the fathers. We regard it as unfortunate that we are still compelled to provide the means of fertilising our wugs, and we look forward to the time when we can dispense with their services."

"But you will still need the services of your wugs, or do you hope to maintain the Lunatic population out of test-tubes?" I asked.

"That should be our ultimate aim," Nob 9 replied.

"And produce a being that is neither mug nor wug?"

"Exactly. But such an achievement seems at present very far away. The problem of producing life out of not-life still baffles our knowalls and we may have to put up with our nine thousand nine hundred and ninety-nine drunes for a long time yet. I shall ask the Office of Drunery to grant special permission for you to visit the Seminary. I shall be anxious to know if our drunes remind you at all of Boojum mugs. I shall say frankly that we do not find them attractive. There was a talkation in Talkery not so long ago to decide whether all our drunes should leave Lunamania when they are forty and retire from active service instead of allowing some of them to remain in Lunamania for another ten years as we do now."

"You will not be allowed to go," the Pantek added, turning to Tod 51. "We do not allow any mugs under a hundred and twenty-one to visit the Seminary and of course no wugs of any age are allowed even to enter the Seminary Reservation." Nob 9 turned to me. "Yes, I shall be interested to hear what you think of our drunes. And now let us look round the Omnibum."

We came out of the Pantek's ritery and took an upstep to the great room at the top of the Omnibum where the task of extracting life out of not-life was being ardently pursued by about a couple of hundred knowalls. Walls and ceilings alike were of sanaton and the first impression was of a crowd of gardeners at work in an immense conservatory. I could see that Tin Pan was much impressed by the outward evidence of diligent, almost feverish experiment and research, but for a technological ignoramus like myself the activity round me was as meaningless as the activity of a disturbed ant-heap.

"Do you think they will ever be successful in extracting life out of not-life?" I asked Tin Pan.

"Nothing is impossible for Science, Mr Bosworth," he affirmed reverently.

"If I could believe that, Mr Tin Pan, I should be able to believe in God. Indeed, I should not find it so very difficult to believe in the Devil." The beginning of a theological discussion between Tin Pan and myself was interrupted by the Pantek.

"Let us now go to see the bookery," he said.

The great library, as we should call it, was a rotunda in the heart of the Omnibum, and I was immediately struck by the convenience for the student of its arrangement. All round at intervals were lifts for a single passenger which took him up to balconies from which he could reach any volume he required. There were also alcoves at intervals among the shelves to which he could retire and study any volume without having to bring it down, for the sake perhaps of a single reference.

"Are there other bookeries in the Lunatic Republic, Nob 9?"

"No, these are all the books and records that we have. After the Abominable War, no books or records of Lunaria remained, and very few of the Lunatian records. Books were given up long ago owing to the scarcity of paper, and although we still call it the bookery of the Omnibum, our shelves are almost entirely filled with the records of the various Management Offices. However, Bosworth One, if you wish to consult the Lunatic chronicles, our bookmugs will give you all the help they can and I am sure you will find much to interest you in the early chronicles. I don't think you will be so much interested in the Management records, which consist almost entirely of statistics about the production of bixifit and that sort of thing. I know that much we deplore nowadays happened in Lunamania once upon a time, and yet, Bosworth One, I shall tell you frankly that there are moments when I sometimes wish I had lived in that Lunamania of long ago."

I told the Pantek that many of us in Boojumania wished the same about the past.

"Mind you, Nob 9, we have not yet reached anything like the almost mechanical perfection of existence which you have attained in the Lunatic Republic, but we are moving in that direction and I think that in another two or three hundred years we shall achieve a good deal of what you achieved long ago. Yet—and I beg you not to think what I am going to say implies the slightest criticism of your way of life—many of us in Boojumania look back to the tales of what life was like once upon a time with a kind of feeling that we are slowly being deprived of what really makes life worth living. Some of us wonder whether the increasing importance we attach to the welfare of the body may not end in destroying what used to be called the soul."

"The soul?" Nob 9 repeated. "We do not have such a word. What does it mean?"

"Many Boojums still believe, in spite of all the evidence our knowalls produce to the contrary, that everybody possesses an immortal soul."

"But what is a soul?" the Pantek asked.

"Those who still believe in the soul declare that within our bodies there dwells an indestructible essence which makes what we call death a mere preliminary to a richer life beyond. I cannot say that I believe in the soul myself, but there are moments when I wish that I could be like those Boojums who still believe in what we call personal immortality. You do not speak of dying. I know that death and dying are words that must not be spoken in the Lunatic Republic, but have you ever wondered, Nob 9, if when you leave Lunamania you will be moving on to an existence elsewhere?"

The Pantek shook his head.

"No, such a thought has never occurred to me."

"But have you ever asked yourself why you should be living at all?"

"We live. That is a fact we cannot deny."

"And you never ask why?"

"No, I never ask why because there cannot be an answer."

"I am almost sure that you are right, Nob 9. But I am not perfectly sure that you are right," I felt suddenly apologetic in the presence of this dignified figure. "I have no business to be talking like this. I think it was your remark that sometimes you wish you had lived in the Lunamania of long ago that set me off. I wondered why you should wish that, living as you do in conditions that must be very much more securely comfortable than those which formerly prevailed in that Lunamania of long ago."

The Pantek and I were alone in his ritery now. Tin Pan had asked Tod 51 to take him up to the great room at the top of the Omnibum where the knowalls were trying to solve the problem of extracting life out of not-life.

"You will regard it as a secret between you and me. Bosworth One, if I tell you something about myself?" the Pantek asked solemnly.

"I shall regard it as a sacred confidence, Nob 9," I assured him with equal solemnity.

"I am approaching the end of my existence on Lunamania. I am told that when I have left I may be accorded an honour which is hardly ever accorded to Lunatics, and that is to be the last holder of the name Nob 9. Nobs will come and Nobs will go, but there will never again be a Nob 9. It may well be that Talkery will not agree that I deserve such an exceptional honour, in which case there will be a mugling called Nob 9 at once, who when he reaches the age of twenty may not be fortunate in the draw and so become a digmug and never become a knowall or even a chair-mug. However, as I say, that will be for Talkery to decide, and in the kindness of oblivion I shall never be aware what Talkery does decide. And indeed when I look back at the fifty years during which I have been Pantek I cannot recall any contribution I have made to the welfare of the Everlasting Lunatic Republic of such signal importance as to justify my name being preserved for myself."

"If I am still in Lunamania when you have left it, I for one shall find it difficult to address another as Nob 9."

"If you are still in Lunamania?" the Pantek asked.

"If you had an opportunity to return to Boojumania, would you accept it?"

"Oh yes, I am sure that I should."

"But from what you have told me about existence in Boojumania, Bosworth One, you would be returning to a much lower form of existence than you have found in the Everlasting Lunatic Republic."

"It may be a less advanced state of lunatisation, Nob 9, but it is a more varied existence, although I should add that existence on Boojumania to-day is not nearly as varied as it was even when I was a boy. You said just now that sometimes you fancied you would have liked to experience the less secure conditions of life in the Lunamania of once upon a time. Why do you ever have such unusual fancies?"

The Pantek paused before he tried to answer my question. Then he shook his head.

"It is perhaps the surprise of the arrival of two Boojums that has stirred me to wish for more surprises, because surprises come so seldom in the Lunatic Republic. There are moments when I am depressed by the regularity of our existence."

"May I make one criticism of your way of life, Nob 9?"

"We speak together in confidence," he replied.

"You have music, but it is only music to which you dance. You have no music to express the hidden emotions and aspirations of lunamanity, and if you tell me that you are the only mug in the Lunatic Republic to have hidden emotions and aspirations I shall find that difficult to believe. And then you have no poetry."

"What is poetry?"

It is difficult enough to define poetry when you have a book of poetry which you can use for illustrations, but to define poetry for a Lunatic was more than I could manage. I tried to think of some poetry I could quote, but I could not think of anything except 'To be or not to be, that is the question', and I did not think an isolated line like that would leave the Pantek much wiser about poetry.

"It's a pity," I said, "that all the Lunarian books were destroyed in the Abominable War. I have a feeling that the old Lunarians may have written poetry."

"Ah, poetry is something that is ritten," the Pantek exclaimed.

I had a shot at trying to explain about rhyme and versification, but the Pantek obviously could not grasp such a use of language.

"Do you write much of what you call poetry in Boojumania?" he asked.

"As a matter of fact, the ability to write it no longer exists. We are now dependent upon the poetry of the past. There was for some time an attempt to make poetry able to deal with modern conditions, but it seldom succeeded in being anything but bad prose."

"Prose?"

"That is the expression for writing what is not verse. And that reminds me. Is it only the writemugs in the Lunatic Republic who can write? Is nobody else taught?"

"What would be the use? Nobody except knowalls can read."

"We are moving in that direction in Boojumania. We still teach our muglings and wuglings to read, but fewer and fewer of them continue to read when they have left school. Hardly any novels are written nowadays."

"Novels?"

"A novel is an imaginary story about imaginary people, but nowadays the newspapers and television, as we call the see-all, can provide all the fiction the public enjoys."

"Fiction?"

"That is another name for novels."

"And newspapers, what are they?" the Pantek asked.

"Once upon a time newspapers which were published every day provided people with news of what was happening all over Boojumania."

"Yes, yes," said the Pantek, "like our bigmouths in the Office of Announcement."

"But nowadays," I went on, "the newspapers leave the news to television and only indulge in gossip to keep people amused when they cannot be looking at television. And of course there is a lot about sport in the newspapers. We are just as keen on sport in Boojumania as you are in the Lunatic Republic. We regard football, which is a game rather like feetball, as one of the greatest deterrents to war. Any government on earth would hesitate before going to war and depriving its people of football."

"I must tell you something, Bosworth One, which I would not tell to any Lunatic . . ." and then the Pantek stopped abruptly. He was evidently debating with himself whether after all he could make the disclosure that he was contemplating. "Do you enjoy sport, Bosworth One?" he enquired at last.

"I enjoy it in moderation," I replied. "But I think one can have too much of it."

"That is what I feel. One can have too much of it, and for many years now I have been feeling that I have had too much of it. But you already know what importance we attach to sameness in the Lunatic Republic, and if at F-time I were to return to the Omnibum instead of going to the gimpasium with my fellow Lunatics, you must already realise that by doing so I should be considered an unusual mug, and to be unusual in the Lunatic Republic is thought to be anti-social and to be anti-social is regarded as not to be all for all, and that is what we call deviation. Do you have that word in Boojumania?"

"We are using it more and more and it is becoming a graver offence all the time. Formerly we spoke of high treason, which meant plotting against the monarch, and when monarchs became fewer and less important, plotting against the government, or management as you say. Nowadays deviation has taken the place of treason."

"And what is a monarch?"

I tried to explain the theory of kingship but this the Pantek found incomprehensible.

"It is really an inherited instead of an elected president," I said.

"But we do not elect our President. It is an office con-ferred by the luck of the draw, and his term of office is only four years."

"We are still electing presidents in Boojumania, but one of the things I most admire in the Lunatic system of Management is your custom of assigning every function to the luck of the draw. If ever I return to Boojumania, I shall devote the rest of my energy to advocating it for us."

"I must remind you," said Nob 9 with a smile, "that there is one exception in the Lunatic Republic. The Pantek is always elected by the knowalls and chair-mugs."

"So I have been told. How do you account for such an exception?"

"It has always been our custom. I suppose that when the Lunatic Republic was struggling to survive after the Abominable War it was necessary to be sure that the direction of the knowalls was in the hands of a recognised knowmost. I have enjoyed our little chatter, Bosworth One, and I hope that from time to time we shall have more little chatters. Your arrival in the Everlasting Lunatic Republic has relieved the sameness which I have been finding sad for some years now. But please never repeat that. Sameness is strength."

I took this opportunity to ask the Pantek if I might be allowed to study the Lunatic chronicles in the bookery of the Omnibum.

"You shall have a ritery for yourself, Bosworth One, and if Tin Pan One desires a ritery he shall have one too. Do not hesitate to consult me when you find yourself perplexed by our chronicles."

At this moment Tod 51 came back with Tin Pan, and my conversation with the Pantek was interrupted, but as he walked with us to the entrance of the Omnibum I was able to assure him that whatever he had said to me would never be repeated.

"And where are you taking our Boojum friends to-morrow?" he asked Tod 51.

"I was thinking of showing them some of the gimpasiums, Nob 9. The Manager of Gimpery wishes to accompany us."

"You will certainly learn all that can be learnt about Gimpery from Bum 444," said the Pantek with what I fancied was almost a sigh of relief that he was not to be one of the party. Then he said quickly, with a glance in my direction, "and I will arrange for our Boojum friends to visit the Seminary soon."

I felt that the Pantek was trying to compensate me for the excess of sport I was in for to-morrow.

## Chapter 10

W E were given a warm welcome by Bum 444 when
Tod 51 took us to the Gimpery Office. The
Manager of Gimpery was obviously much gratified by
the prospect of personally conducting us round some
of the gimpasiums.

"And you will find that I am not such a useless mug,"
he said with a grin. He had remembered what his name
meant to Boojums and it may have rankled. No, that is
not fair; nothing ever seems to rankle with anybody in
the Lunatic Republic.

"But before we leave Gimpery let us see the presentation of the muglings three months old who arrived in
Lunamania after the six-months carry-time."

There were half a dozen wugs with three-month old
muglings in their arms who were waiting in the examination room for the arrival of the knowalls qualified to
decide whether these candidates for gimpery were
eligible. One who had arrived only two minutes over
normal carry-time was rejected, and then lots were
drawn for the two gimper vacancies. As soon as their
future was decided, the two gimperlings, as they were
now called, were taken away from their mothers by
two rearwugs who would superintend the diet and look
after their gimperling charges until at four years old
their training to become gimpers would begin.

"Are gimper-drunes fed on a special vitalot that
enables them to produce gimpers?"

"That is true," said Bum 444, "but it is not considered
desirable for the wugs to know which of them have been
drunified by gimper-drunes. Therefore a surplus of
wugs are thus drunified and the muglings are always

over five minutes late, but when they are less than five minutes late the muglings are rejected for gimpery, to guard against the possibility of an error of judgment."

"Have mistakes ever been made?"

"Once or twice," Bum 444 admitted with obvious unwillingness. "That is why we insist on a minimum of five minutes over carry-time."

"But what happens to the rejected gimper-mugilng? And to those who are unsuccessful in the draw?"

"They remain with their mothers until they are two years old and then instead of going to school they leave Lunamania. The selected gimperlings are given the vitalots necessary for them to become gimpers."

"But how are muglings able to chew the necessary vitalots?" I asked.

"Why can they not chew?"

"Surely they are not born with teeth?" I exclaimed.

"Not born with teeth?" Bum 444 repeated in amazement. "How else could they bite the mother-cord when they arrive in Lunamania?"

"But how can their mothers suckle them if they are born with teeth?"

"What is 'suckle'?"

I gave as lucid a description as could be expected from a bachelor of the suckling of a human infant, and my description of the process shocked Bum 444 and Tod 51 as profoundly as it would shock a he-man in America to find that the nipples on his hairy chest were milk-conductors.

"That is the most unlunatised thing I have ever heard," Bum 444 declared.

When the Manager of Gimpery had recovered from my revelation about the way human mothers nurture their babies, we paid a visit to the hive where the first five years of a gimper's life are spent in the care of rear-

F

mugs whose business it is, besides administering the vitalots that develop the bodily growth of the gimperling, to discourage at the same time any premature mental growth—because it is believed that activity of the brain may militate against physical training. Muglings and wuglings ordinarily go to school when they are two years old and remain there until they are twenty, when, as I have mentioned already, lots are drawn to decide which muglings shall continue for another ten years in order to become knowalls and chairmugs and which shall proceed immediately to perform the manual labour of the Lunatic Republic.

There was nothing of interest in the hive where the gimperlings pass the first five years of their lives, and I was glad when we left it for what is called First Trainery to which the gimperlings go when it is time to begin their long, and as we were to find out, arduous training.

The gimperlings in First Trainery spend the first five years of their time in walking and running forwards and backwards under the direction of senior gimpertrainers whose age may be as much as a hundred and sixty. These trainers all had blue beards; the younger ones of a hundred and twenty had short ultramarine beards and those of a hundred and fifty and over had much longer light blue beards. I asked when hair grew on the faces of gimpers and was told that it began to grow when they retired from the ballroom, the racing track and the kikwik-ring.

"If a Lunatic mug chewed enough gimper vitalots, would hair grow on his face?" I asked.

Bum 444 could not answer this question. The unlunatised idea of anybody except a gimper chewing enough gimper vitalots to grow hair on his face was beyond his imagination.

At fifteen the gimperlings move on to Second

Trainery, where for another ten years they practise running, bounding, kikwikery and squeezery. Then at twenty-five, having passed from being gimperlings to being gimperlets, they enter Third Trainery and begin feetball, to excel at which when they become gimpers at the age of forty is the main object of a gimper's life, and which he will continue to play for the next eighty years for the diversion of the Lunatic population at F-time. I began to realise why the Pantek, tired of countless feetball matches, sighed for that Lunamania of long ago, even if the way of life there had led ultimately to the Abominable War.

I must admit that I was pretty bored myself by the time we had visited one trainery after another and one gimpasium after another. However, there was one exercise for squeezing in Second Trainery which was out of the usual. This consisted of burying half a dozen gimperlings about five feet deep and seeing which of them reappeared above ground first.

"This is a very good exercise to keep the breath," said Bum 444. "And the great art of squeezery is to keep the breath longer than your opponent. Squeezery used to be called throwabout, and of course as you have seen there is still much throwabout in it; but it was found that the mugs and wugs enjoyed most of all that part of throwabout when the two throwers, as they used to be called, were squeezing each other for the victory. So it was decided by Talkery that the name throwabout should be given up and that in future it should be called squeezery and that the throwers should be called squeezers."

We stood watching the ground heave as the gimperlings struggled to unearth themselves until at last they emerged, all of them indigo in the face with their efforts not to be suffocated. I asked if this tough exercise had ever been too much for any of those taking part in it.

"Yes, once or twice gimperlings have had to leave Lunamania in a hurry," Bum 444 replied. "But it was better for them that they should do that rather than disgrace themselves in the gimpasium. To be squeezed out of Lunamania in the middle of a squeezing match would be a terrible disgrace."

"And that has never happened?"

"It may have happened in the past; it has never happened in my time, and I am now a hundred and forty-two," said the Manager of Gimpery, swelling slightly with the consciousness of the important position he enjoyed in the Lunatic Republic.

While we were on the subject of leaving Lunamania I thought I would enquire about funeral customs. Bum 444 was obviously shocked to hear about ours on earth.

"You bury them in the ground or you burn them, in Boojumania?" he exclaimed. "That is a very unlunatised way of treating what you call the remains of those who have left Boojumania. Why are there any remains? When a Lunatic comes to a hundred and ninety-nine he does not know that he has come to the end of his age because no Lunatic knows the exact day when he arrived in Lunamania. Only the Office of Arrival and Departure knows that. Lunatics in their last year know that the time to leave is approaching because all those in their last year eat together in the hives of departure, although they keep their cells in the hives where they have spent their time in Lunamania after leaving school and they always return to them at K-time to sleep. Then after the Office of Arrival and Departure has notified the hives of departure which mugs or wugs will be leaving Lunamania in the night they are given a devitalot at Third Eat. When they come back at K-time, they are seen to have turned white and in the morning there is a little dust in each of their beds. This is put into a small box by one of the Arrival and Departure chairmugs and taken to the Office. Then the muglings and wuglings who arrive in Lunamania that day are given by Arrival and Departure the names of those who have left. It is all very simple."

"But what happens to the dust of those who have left?"

"A chairmug at Arrival and Departure gives it to a digmug, and he scatters it among the bixifit growth. It is not a heavy task. Only twenty-five mugs and wugs leave Lunamania every night."

"Not much ancestor worship in the Lunatic Republic," I observed to Tin Pan.

"We discourage it now in the Celestial Chinese Republic, Mr Bosworth," he assured me. "We believe that we honour our ancestors best by the perfection of our corporate life to-day."

Various gimpers were presented to us in the course of our tour of the gimpasiums; the discouragement of personalifikation being always in mind, their athletic feats were not mentioned except in one case. This was Gimper 1066 of First Lunatic Town, who had just won the five-oop race against the other eight Lunatic Towns and who in another month would be competing against the five-oop champion of Lunatic City.

We saw him in a five-oop training race at the First Town gimpasium, by which I was as much baffled as Alice by the caucus race in Wonderland. The runners started off like ordinary runners and then after about a minute ran backwards for twice as long. Then they all began to run in different directions for several minutes until a whistle blew, whereupon they all ran backwards towards a pole striped with royal blue and carmine, the First Lunatic Town colours, that stood in the middle of the ballroom, as it may be remembered the arena is called. The gimper who first touches the pole with his back then has to swarm up to the top of it, and if he can stay there, against every attempt by the other gimpers to pull him off, until the whistle blows again he is declared to have won not the race, as I expected, but only the first oop. Then comes the second oop. This time the runners start off backwards, and when they have gone once round the track they begin running about in all directions until the whistle blows, when they all run forwards to the pole and then run round it until the whistle sounds again when for no reason that I could divine one of them is declared to have won the second oop. And so the five-oop race continues, getting more and more difficult to understand all the time. The only race on earth that is equally difficult for the spectator to follow is a sailing-race. Yet I have to admit that the ordinary spectator in the Lunatic Republic seems perfectly able to follow oop-racing.

It was when the practice for the coming championship was over that the Manager of Gimpery could not resist presenting to us Gimper 1066 of Lunatic First Town.

"This is Gimper 1066, who will be a representative of the Nine Towns against Lunatic City in the five-oop championship next month."

Tin Pan and I made the conventional gesture of greeting as naturally as if we had been living in the Lunatic Republic for years, and Gimper 1066 responded with obvious pleasure. No doubt, in spite of the danger of personalifikation, he would get a good deal of kudos when the gimpers gathered at E-time for Second Eat.

"Our Gimpery officer in First Town," said Bum 444, "told me that Gimper 1805, the leader of the feetball twenty-five, had been chattering about seeing two

Boojums so near to him when he was congratulated by the President last week. He thought it would be valuable if Gimper 1066 could chatter as much, in case Gimper 1805 should be tempted to be at all puffish."

I think this was probably an excuse. I fancy Bum 444 as a First Town hiver himself was indulging in a bit of favouritism, for I know he was delighted when the President congratulated Gimper 1805 after the feetball match. When we visited the gimpasium in Lunatic Ninth Town Bum 444 asked us if we should like to join the gimpers at Second Eat, and I hastily expressed our pleasure at the idea, for by now I was feeling hungry. The gimper table was the right height for Tin Pan and me, but Bum 444's legs were dangling above the floor and once or twice I thought he was going to topple off the bench on which we were sitting.

The meal began with bixifit, but the vitalots had a different colour and taste from any of those we had in our hive, being a vivid crimson with a flavour which reminded me now of pineapple, now of onions, and occasionally of syrup of figs into which somebody had spilt soapy water. When analysed like that, the flavour does not sound particularly attractive, but when one says that the durian of Malaya tastes like a mixture of strawberries and cream, Irish stew and paraffin, that does not sound attractive, and yet it is in fact delicious.

I asked Bum 444 what would be the effect on us of eating the gimper vitalots every day.

"We could not do it," he told me, "We cannot have the activation which the gimper vitalots demand."

And certainly when we left the Ninth Town gimpasium and went up on the self-walk to return to Lunatic City I did feel a great desire to run with it instead of to walk with it in the recognised style of Lunatic progress.

"You will be seeing the squeezery matches between Lunatic City and Lunatic Fifth Town at F-time," Bum 444 reminded us.

And perhaps under the influence of that crimson vitalot I danced a gleeful assent. Yet at the back of my mind I felt I had had quite enough sport for the day and should have liked to go along to the Omnibum and enjoy another quiet chat with the Pantek who had grown a little tired of sport in the course of his hundred and ninety-one years.

After we had parted from Bum 444 with our thanks for giving us such an interesting lookabout, as a tour is called in Lunatic, we got on the downstep leading from the self-walk to the gimpasium. Suddenly I heard my name called and turned to see the beaming face of Pup 301. Readers may wonder why I was able to recognise him immediately. I remind them that every Lunatic has his name and number embroidered upon his upper garment.

"Ah, how glad I am to meet you, Bosworth One," he exclaimed. "And you too, Tin Pan One. I will not intrude if I sit with you to see the squeezery?"

Pup 301 glanced at Tod 51.

"Certainly you do not intrude, Pup 301," said Tod 51 cordially.

I may mention as a most agreeable characteristic of Lunatic life the entire absence of jealousy. Not once since I have lived in the Lunatic Republic have I seen the slightest sign of it either among the ordinary mugs and wugs or, more remarkably to us human beings, among the official class.

Pup 301 was now a pink, having been promoted by the President to be a first-class lookmug and appointed to the staff of the Lookalty, and he was wearing the Pink Star, being, it may be remembered, at the age of ninety-five the youngest mug in the Lunatic Republic to receive such an honour.

"The First Look of the Lookalty was wondering when you were bringing our Boojum guests to pay us a visit?" Pup 301 said to our guide.

"Why, it is strange you should say that," said Tod 51, "for I was planning to bring them to the Lookalty to-morrow if it was convenient for the First Look to receive them."

"It will be highly convenient at D-time to-morrow because Cod 678 intends to inspect the new look-house we have built close to where that Boojum roundabout came down with what we thought was a Boojum mug-ling inside, but which we have now been informed by the Karetaker of the Kurarium is a creature called a monkey. . . ." Pup 301 broke off to look at me to confirm that he had the name right.

"That is so," I assured him.

By this time we had reached the stand where two higher seats were always reserved for Tin Pan and myself, and for the rest of F-time we watched the squeezery. I am sure that my unimaginable readers will have had enough of sport for the present and indeed I had had so much of it during our lookabout of the gimpasiums that after G-time in the chatterbox at Hive 6 I asked Tod 51 if it would be considered a breach of etiquette for me to miss the see-all in the sittery at H-time and invite Pup 301 up to my cell for a chatter.

Tod 51 hesitated for a moment before he replied.

"I think it will be all right," he finally decided. "Pup 301 is a pink and the hivers will think that he wants to chatter to you about official business."

So after woo-hoo had sounded for the hivers to go up to the sittery, Pup 301 and I stayed on the upstep until we reached the floor where my cell was. We invited Tin

F*

Pan to come along too, but he said he thought he would lie down until Third Eat. Tod 51 had left at H-time after telling Pup 301 that we should arrive at the Lookalty at D-time.

"The First Look will be very pleased. If I am lucky, perhaps he will invite me to come too," said Pup 301.

"Now that you have been for a little while in the Lunatic Republic, are you happy, Bosworth One?" my first friend on the Moon asked when we were alone in my cell.

"I am much happier, Pup 301, than I should ever have believed possible when our fizzer came down at the edge of the Great Lunarian Waste, and I want to tell you how grateful I am to you for the tactful way in which you introduced us to the Lunatic Republic."

"I merely did what any mug would have done," said Pup 301.

"But I think you would not now be wearing that Pink Star unless the President had recognised the remarkable way in which you handled a situation unique in the history of the Lunatic Republic. I think you are too modest."

"It was a lucky day for me when we saw you and Tin Pan One walking towards the look-house. Thanks to you, I am now a pink at the Lookalty and I can wear this."

He touched the Pink Star on his upper garment with reverence.

"And what that you have seen here has impressed you most?" he asked.

"Impressions have crowded upon me so fast that each fresh one seems more remarkable than the last. But I think I remember with most warmth of feeling the kindness of your President and the charm of his mother, Sex 715. I am looking forward with intense expectation to meeting her again next week. I hear she is giving a party for us to meet some of her wug friends who wish to hear more about what we call fashions in Boojumania."

"Fashions?" Pup 301 repeated.

"It is a wuggish subject," I said quickly; I did not want to involve myself in trying to explain to Pup 301 something which he would not be able to comprehend. So to change the chatter I told him what a profound impression the Pantek had made upon me.

"Yes, that is indeed a wonderful mug," he exclaimed with enthusiasm. "All of us in the Lunatic Republic are in admiration of Nob 9 and sad to think that he will be leaving Lunamania eight years hence. We feel that there can never again be a Nob 9, and there is already chatter that perhaps Talkery will pass an Action for no mugling ever again to be called Nob 9."

"What is he particularly admired for?" I asked.

"He is most admired because when the first fizzer came from Boojumania he was able to persuade Talkery not to pass an Action for us to start building fizzers in the Lunatic Republic."

"He was indeed far-sighted," I said, "for I am sure if the Lunatic Republic had started to build fizzers such a policy would have ended in sending fizzers to Boojumania and the people in Boojumania would have declared that they were being threatened by Lunamania and ultimately all the resources of both would have been wasted in building bigger and better fizzers until Boojumania and Lunamania wouldn't have been able to resist finding out which had the biggest and the best."

"The arrival of you and Tin Pan One has had a good effect," Pup 301 assured me. "The hivers in Hive 6 have spread everywhere the news that you are both very lunatised, and all Lunatics rejoice that Talkery agreed to grant you the hospitality of our Everlasting Republic."

"For which we have first you to thank, Pup 301, and then the President."

"You have nothing to thank me for, Bosworth One, but when you thank the President, you must thank also the Pantek. I have heard since from my colleagues at the Lookalty that the President consulted with the Pantek before the orders were given that you were to come as soon as possible to the Pink House. You remember when Tin Pan One was stuck to the silon gate?"

"I do indeed."

"The order of the Lookalty is that if any Boojums arrive in Lunamania they are to stick to the fence until they leave Lunamania. I did not disobey the order because Tin Pan One was stuck to the gate not to the fence. I informed the First Look of this on the quick-speak. He then consulted the Pantek and the Pantek went to the Pink House, after which the President authorised me to bring you into Lunatic City."

When Pup 301 had gone away to his own hive, I stayed in my cell until the woo-hoo sounded for Third Eat, thinking to myself about all the stupid statesmen and politicians of the twentieth century—British, German, French, Russian, Italian, American and the rest—who had led the world almost to the brink of annihilation during a century which had added more to human knowledge than any previous century and might by the second millennium have seen all mankind moving confidently toward a hitherto unimaginable condition of happiness and prosperity. Would the Chinese in the twenty-first century succeed in achieving what the West had failed to achieve in the twentieth century? I looked back at my experience in Peking. There was not much sign of moral improvement yet, and however confidently Tin Pan might argue I was not convinced that there was much sign of mental improvement; I wondered if I were to return to Earth what I should feel about humanity after my experience of lunamanity. At this point in my highly inconclusive reflections the woo-hoo sounded and I hurried along to the downstep with pleasant anticipation of the bixifit I should munch at Third Eat.

Next morning Tod 51 came along to take us to the Lookalty, where the First Look expressed his pleasure at the prospect of our accompanying him on his visit of inspection to the new look-house where the Russian roundabout had come down with the monkey inside.

Cod 678 introduced us to Vim 40, the Second Look, who I had been told by Pup 301 was one of those in the Lunatic Management that doubted the wisdom of refusing to build counterfizzers to defend Lunamania against an attack by Boojum fizzers and roundabouts. Vim 40 questioned me closely about the reason for sending Tin Pan and myself to Lunamania.

"It was curiosity, Vim 40," I insisted firmly. "Our Boojum knowalls, who have a clear idea about the side of Lunamania they can see, wanted to be sure that the other side invisible from Boojumania was essentially the same. They know nothing about the Everlasting Lunatic Republic. If the instruments in our fizzer had not failed to function, we should have been able to tell them about the Lunatic Republic, and I can assure you, Vim 40, that the last thing we should contemplate in Boojumania would be an attack on such a lunatised society. What could possibly be gained by such an attack?"

"What could possibly be gained by the Lunarians three thousand years ago from attacking Lunatia? Nevertheless, they did attack it, and in consequence practically the whole of Lunamania is to-day an uninhabitable desert."

"With all deference, Vim 40, I do not think the case is parallel. I have not yet been able to study at all thoroughly the Lunatic chronicles preserved in the Omnibum, but I understand that there were various grounds for enmity between Lunaria and Lunatia because each suspected the other of trying to impose a way of life of which neither approved. We are unfortunately still to a large extent in that condition in Boojumania, though happily not to the same extent as we were forty years ago. Therefore we are far too much occupied with our own problems of survival to have any aggressive designs upon Lunamania."

"But it might be to the advantage of one of the ways of life to seek the help of the Lunatic Republic to overpower the other," said the Second Look, gazing at me intently from his bright little eyes.

"Such an idea could hardly occur to people who have no notion that such a highly lunatised Management as the Lunatic Republic exists, and surely, Vim 40, the Lunatic Republic would never treat such a proposal with anything but the contempt it deserves."

"Come, come, Vim 40," said the First Look with an amicable grin, "do not try to upset Bosworth One with your fancifikations."

"If they *are* fancifikations," said the Second Look gloomily. "They may be practikalities, Cod 678."

"The Second Look is much more worried about your Boojum fizzers than the rest of us," Pup 301 said to me as we were walking with the self-walk towards the new look-house, which I was a little disappointed to find lay in the opposite direction from the look-house which Tin Pan and I had reached from Heavenly Dragon with such relief. I had hoped that we might be allowed through the magnetised silon fence which bars the Lunatics from a sight of Earth shining sapphirine in a jet-black sky amid myriads of ineffably bright stars. However, it was not to be. We remained under the synthetic sky of the Lunatic Republic as we passed the hives of Fourth Lunatic Town and Fifth Lunatic Town and many acres of bixifit to the new look-house, the chief feature of which was a powerful looking-glass, or tele-scope as we say, giving a wonderful view of the foothills that led to the range of mighty mountains along the horizon. Apart from this, the Roundabout Look-house as it was called did not differ from what we learnt had now been re-named the Boojum Look-house, where Pup 301 and his patrol had received us on that memorable night of our arrival. Oh yes, brushabouts had been introduced here, so that the spectacle of the lookmugs brushing one another at K-time would no longer be seen by any future visitors from the Earth. There was a similar eatery and a similar sleepery to those in the Boojum Look-house, and of course the same sanaton transparency instead of earthly bricks and mortar in the construction. A similar patrol of Tweedledums and Tweedledees was on guard, commanded by a lookmug called Tod 251; this was the first time I had come across a duplication of one of the names, which was surprising because each of them belonged to nine hundred and ninety-nine mugs and wugs, so that there were many more numbers than names.

The First Look said he should like to see the place where the roundabout with the monkey had come down. So Tod 251 gave the order to demagnetise the silon gate and we all walked along the roadway which led toward the foothills. As we were on our way, a ludicrous incident occurred. The lookmug whose turn it was to remagnetise the silon gate when we had passed through was a recruit to the status of lookmug; indeed, according to Tod 251 he had still been a digmug only last week. It may be remembered that when Tin Pan hurried to examine more closely the substance called silon he was stuck to the gate until Pup 301 stood upon the lid of something like a manhole beside the road to demagnetise the gate and release him. Instead of standing on the demagnetising lid, the lookmug newcomer stood on another lid which shut off the keepdown. The result was that all of us who were on the road beyond the gate suddenly found ourselves bouncing about all over the place like rubber balls. It was certainly an extraordinary sensation and, none of us being trained gimpers, we could not control our movements. I lost my gravity in both meanings of the word, for as I bounced about I could not help laughing at the indignant expression on the faces of the First Look and the Second Look as they bounced about just as helplessly.

Tod 251 made a valiant effort to bounce in the direction of the gate, but before he could reach it another lookmug in the patrol had had the presence of mind to stand on the lid that turned on the keepdown.

"What is the name of the lookmug who shut off the keepdown?" the First Look demanded sternly when Tod 251 regained the party of inspection.

"His name is Vim 400," replied Tod 251 with an apprehensive glance at Vim 40.

"What?" the Second Look shouted, furious that a lookmug capable of such stupidity should have so nearly the same name as himself. Then he turned to the First Look. "This boojumatic is not fit to be a lookmug."

"He has only been a lookmug for a week," Tod 251 explained. "It was the first time he has had to work the gate and his brainpot must have cracked."

"He should be sent back to diggery," said Vim 40 with a glance at Cod 678.

The First Look had been displeased by the Second

Look's calling Vim 400 a boojumatic. He felt that the use of this Lunatic word for an imbecile was discourteous to his Boojum guests. Moreover, I fancy he felt that the Second Look was inclined to be a bit puffish. Anyway, he said to Tod 251, "You will rebuke Vim 400 and warn him that if such a mistake is made again he will be sent back to diggery. And now let us proceed."

"The First Look is a very all-round mug," Tod 51 observed to me as we were walking along. "He knows that Tod 251 was not able to order another lookmug to work the gate because it was the turn of Vim 400, and they are stricter about turns at the Lookalty than we are in the Home Management Office."

I guessed that an all-round mug meant what we should call a fair-minded man.

"And he was not pleased when the Second Look called Vim 400 a boojumatic."

"I felt that. But it's quite natural that you Lunatics should speak of boojumatics because . . ."

I was abruptly silent.

"Because what?" Tod 51 asked.

I decided to be frank.

"Because we use the word 'lunatic' in exactly the same sense as you use 'boojumatic'."

"Is that so?"

Tod 51 was unimpressed. He obviously thought that such a sense of language was only one more instance of the depths of ignorance in which we Boojums existed.

By now we were drawing near to the spot where the Russian roundabout had fallen in a rocky waste; the great mountain range rose before us and behind us shimmered the domes of the Lunatic Republic.

"No fizzers have come down on this side of Lunamania, have they?" I asked.

"Not yet," the Second Look replied, and I fancied

from the tone of his voice that if a fizzer did come down on this side of the moon the Pantek, and those in accord with the policy he advocated of refusing to build counter-fizzers with which to retaliate, might find the opposition to that policy much stronger that it was at present.

That fancy was confirmed when we were walking with the self-walk back to Lunatic City and Pup 301 murmured to me "I wonder if the Pantek *is* right."

"I'm quite sure he is right," I said earnestly. "And if you were a Boojum, Pup 301, you would be as sure as I am that he is right."

## Chapter 11

ABOUT a week after our visit to the Roundabout Look-house with the First Look of the Lookalty Tin Pan and I received an invitation from the President's mother to a party at the Pink House. It was brought to Hive 6 by one of her waitmugs whose name was Gal. I was amused by this and omitted to make a note of her number.

"Sex 715 asks if Bosworth One and Tin Pan One will join her in the bowery at G-time to-morrow to meet a party of wugs who are anxious to hear about wuggishness in Boojumania," said Gal in the slow careful speech of somebody who has learnt her message by heart.

"Please tell Sex 715 that Tin Pan One and Bosworth One have the greatest pleasure in accepting her kind invitation to the bowery to-morrow."

Gal looked a little bewildered by the phrasing of my reply.

"It is 'yes'?" she asked doubtfully.

"It is certainly 'yes'."

And as Gal left Hive 6 with our acceptance of Sex 715's invitation, I felt that the only word of it she would take back to the Pink House was 'yes'.

I asked Sex 715 later if my intuition had been right.

"Gal has only said 'yes'," the President's mother told me. "But that was all I wanted to know."

With the prospect of the party I should have been glad to miss going to the gimpasium at F-time, but the worship of sport is so devout in the Lunatic Republic that I feared it might create a bad impression if Tin Pan and I did not attend the bounding match between Lunatic City and Second Lunatic Town; and indeed I must admit that it was a truly remarkable exhibition of athletic skill, of which perhaps the high-light was a backward long bound of over fifty feet by one of the Second Lunatic Town bounders.

When we arrived at the Pink House the doormug who admitted us led us first to the shakery, where after a moment or two Dad 333 came in and gave us a most kindly welcome.

"I hear everywhere how quickly you have taken to our Lunatic way of life and I am very pleased that you have already become quite lunatised. That is good. I wanted to see you before you went to the bowery to tell you that I shall be glad if you will take Third Eat with me at I-time. I have invited the Pantek."

This was indeed an evening to look forward to, and I think the President knew that, judging by the twinkle in his benevolent eyes.

"And now you must go along to the party where the wugs will have many questions to ask about Boojumania." He pressed one of the buttons of his desk for a waitwug to come and conduct us to the bowery, where Sex 715 had invited about twenty wugs, both pinks and blues, to meet us.

I was delighted to see the President's mother again, and when she opened her arms with the conventional gesture of greeting from a wug to a mug it was all I could do to stop short at the conventional response of only appearing to hasten within the embrace, so cordial was her reception of us.

"I am very pleased to see you this G-time, Bosworth One and Tin Pan One," she said, "and I wish to present you to some of my wug friends both young and old."

The wugs all opened their arms, to which we responded with an aplomb I never expected that either of us would achieve so soon.

The Lunatic wugs are not beautiful by our earthly standards as yet, although with the speed modern painting is advancing yearly along the path of ugliness I believe that in another few years a gathering of Lunatic wugs might be serious competitors in our earthly beauty competitions.

Nevertheless, in spite of what I with my old-fashioned notions still consider a lack of facial charm, the whole effect of this wug gathering was almost attractive, with its combination of pink and blue clothes and the various shades of blue in the faces and hands. On earth beauty belongs more to youth than to age, but in the Lunatic Republic the vivid ultramarine of youthful cheeks is less agreeable to the earthly eye than the cobalt of age.

The two or three wuglings not yet thirty years old, whose virginal status was notified by the short skirts they wore instead of the plus-fours of mature wuggishness, had been invited to the party for a special purpose. That talk we had had about fashions with the President's mother had evidently made a deep impression upon her, and I was invited to give what amounted to a lecture on the varieties of the spoon in Boojumania. Spoon, it may be remembered, is the Lunatic name for skirt.

My discourse was received with rapt attention, though I have no doubt it would have been contemptuously dismissed if my audience had consisted of women instead of wugs. My description of the crinoline evoked a babble of incredulous ejaculations; finally Sex 715 made one of the wuglings stand in the middle of the room in order that I might walk round her to demonstrate the width of the crinoline in its prime. Another bit of Boojum costume that fascinated these wugs was the bustle, and I must confess to a faint embarrassment when I was called upon to raise the skirt of another wugling summoned to serve as a model and try to estimate the extent of the protuberance artifically secured. The brassière was beyond the comprehension of my audience because wugs have as little breast as a five-year-old child, and a wug has no more hesitation in exposing it than a schoolboy.

My audience was definitely disappointed when I informed them that there was an ever-growing tendency in Boojumania for our wugs to wear forks instead of spoons, though this was mitigated by my telling them that when our wugs first experimented with forks they wore forks not unlike those worn by the Lunatic wugs but that nowadays Boojum forks were growing tighter every year. I went on to speak of shorts and of their extreme shortness in contemporary Boojumania. This did not please my audience. They could not understand why when the Boojum wugs were able to wear so many different kinds of clothes they should want to get rid of them.

After I had finished speaking, Tin Pan started a little homily about the efforts made by the Celestial Chinese Republic to discourage extravagance in dress, but Sex 715's guests and Sex 715 herself had been much more interested to hear about the extravagance of Boojum ways than about their austerity. They had jumped about and clapped their hands when I finished speaking; there was not a single jump to acclaim Tin Pan.

At this point three waitwugs came into the bowery with trays of a rose-coloured vitalot, the appearance of which was hailed by the guests with an unanimous 'goo-goo!' of pleasurable anticipation. This was Vitalot 12, which the hivers of First Lunatic Town had been given at Third Eat to celebrate their feetball victory over Lunatic City. The President had suggested then that Tin Pan and I should be given them also, but Tod 51 had felt it would make us appear unusual at our first meeting with the hivers of Hive 6 and had suggested we should wait for another festive occasion when everybody in the company would be enjoying Vitalot 12.

Vitalot 12, the prime dainty of the Lunatic Republic, certainly deserves the esteem in which it is held. I make allowances for the likelihood of anything in the Lunatic diet that tastes of something seeming more delicious than it really is, but having tasted the crimson gimper vitalot which I had greatly enjoyed I found Vitalot 12 even more agreeable. At one moment I was reminded of pâté de foie gras, at another of peaches, and somehow these two flavours were blended with olives and oysters to which was added an elusive but most delectable mixture of black currants, marzipan, musk and Camembert cheese. There was no 'chew-hew' formality. The trays were handed round three times for the guests to help themselves, and when they were empty all the wugs jumped about patting their paunches in exhilarated appreciation of the treat they had been given.

The hostess now rose to address the company.

"Wugs of the Everlasting Lunatic Republic, I know I am speaking for all of you when I say how much obliged we are to Bosworth One, our welcome visitor from Boojumania, for the eloquent account he has given us this G-time of Boojum fashions. Fashion is not a Lunatic word, and I never expected at my age to learn a new word which I believe would be a valuable addition to the many valuable words we already possess.

"I shall be leaving Lunamania thirteen years hence and perhaps it is too late at my age to plead for a change in Lunatic ways, but I recall that when I was a wugling I heard Mum 623 speak in this bowery to a gathering of wugs on the need for us to wear footboxes with high stumps that would make us as tall as mugs."

"I was there, I was there," cried an elderly wug called Nut 5. "It was the beginning of one of the greatest reforms the Everlasting Lunatic Republic has known in all its long history."

I asked if I might say something, and when Sex 715 had graciously beckoned me to my feet I told the gathering how much I had been moved to hear that Mum was the name of the great wug who had first put forward the idea that wugs should wear footboxes with stumps and thus put themselves on a level with mugs.

"In the part of Boojumania where I come from Mum is almost a sacred name because it is the intimate diminutive for a word that all Lunatics revere, the word 'mother'. When on the very first day of my arrival in the Everlasting Lunatic Republic I heard your beloved President address our gracious hostess of this G-time as 'mother' I no longer felt a stranger in a strange world. I felt at home. Forgive me, Sex 715, for interrupting what you were going to say, but when you mentioned Mum 623 I was impelled to speak."

"I am glad that you told us what Mum means in Boojumania, Bosworth One," said our hostess. "It gives me courage to say what I wish to say this G-time. The proposal that wugs should wear footboxes with stumps high enough to make them level with mugs was passed by an Action of Talkery exactly a hundred years ago. I was then only eighty-six years old and my son Dad 333 was a chairmug in the Office of Home Management. But I shall remind you that the struggle for wugs to wear separate footboxes with high stumps, instead of the legging-extensions without stumps that the mugs wear, lasted for more than fifty years, and it was not until we threatened to persuade all wuglings to refuse drunifika-tion that Talkery at last surrendered. And never forget that it was only after wugs had footboxes and stumps to put them on a level with mugs that wugs became eligible to draw for membership of Talkery.

"I am now going to propose that we should consider the question of giving up the forks we wear at present and substituting for them a variety of spoons. I do not suggest that we should go to the extremes of fashion in which Bosworth One tells us that Boojum wugs have indulged. I do not think that this large spoon called a crinoline should be adopted by us because it would undoubtedly cause obstruction on the self-walk and indeed Bosworth One has told us that conditions in the Boojumania of to-day are not favourable to the wearing of crinolines. What applies to the crinoline in the way of obstruction applies in a lesser degree to the bustle. If our great project is to be brought to a successful conclusion we must be very careful not to provide the faintest excuse for the mug M.T.s to oppose it in Talkery.

"My own idea is that instead of giving up the spoon when we cease to be wuglings we should retain it and that every year the length of it should be changed by a nail or two so that we can always be in the fashion, as Bosworth One puts it."

Sex 715's proposal was received with enthusiasm. All the wugs in the bowery jumped about and clapped their hands as hard as they could. One wug in her excitement jumped upon a rocking-chair to shout 'up spoons and down forks' and came down herself with a crash. The wugs crowded round me to ask question after question about fashions. They were all anxious, too, to know what *their* names meant in Boojumania. Some were easy enough to translate, of course; some like Nit, Rat and Sow were less easy, and some were impossible. After all, some English monosyllables still do remain impossible in conversation at a tea-party, in spite of the exhibitionist efforts of a few American and British authors to make them sound as harmless as baby talk.

It was half-way through H-time before the guests of

Sex 715 made their farewells. I had rather hoped that the President would join the party, because I wanted to know if these wugs would make their farewells by turning their backs and bending over to salute him through their legs. When they had departed I ventured to ask my hostess if it was customary for wugs to give the same presidential salute as the mugs gave. How she laughed!

"Oh, why didn't you ask me that before the wugs went away, Bosworth One?" she gasped from excess of merriment. "We should have had the best giggle we have had for years. No, no, when a wug salutes the President in farewell she puts both hands behind her head and bows. And now I shall leave you and Tin Pan One to look at the see-all while I go and tell the President about my plan for dress reform. He may ask you some questions about wuggish fashions in Boojumania when you are chattering together after Third Eat, and you must try to get the Pantek interested. He has much influence with the President."

When we gathered in the shakery before Third Eat we found that, besides the Pantek, Dad 333 had invited the Manager of Drunery to meet us. I was tickled to hear that the latter's name was Pop 899: it seemed suitable for the mug who was in control of nine thousand nine hundred and ninety-nine unknown fathers.

"Well, I hear you have been inspiring my mother to propose a revolutionary change in wuggish dress, Bosworth One?" the President said when we were sitting with him in his chatterbox after Third Eat.

His voice sounded grave, but there was a twinkle in his benevolent eye which was reassuring.

"I heard of the proposal of Sex 715 with sympathy," the Pantek said. "It would not do of course to allow this . . ." he paused a moment to pass me a piece of what I shall still call paper (although it is more like vellum than paper) on which he had written 'fashun'. "That is the Boojum word, is it not?" he asked.

Naturally I did not complicate my answer by telling the Pantek that we spelt it 'fashion'.

"I have been reflecting during Third Eat about this idea of fashun," he continued, "and I have come to the conclusion that the admirable system of rules we have built up in the Everlasting Lunatic Republic for the last three thousand years must have been originally inspired by fashun. If a sufficient number of wug M.T.s are prepared to support the proposal of Sex 715, I am willing to put it before a select committee of knowalls in the Omnibum, and should they, as I think they will, decide to make a recommendation to Talkery, I hope that Talkery will pass an Action to allow our Lunatic wugs to wear spoons instead of forks and to regulate their length by means of a committee of fashun wugs chosen by the usual method of the draw. I have not forgotten the endless talkations that went on for over fifty years before Talkery agreed that wugs should have foot-boxes and stumps."

"And I have not forgotten," said Pop 899, "that a year or two later wugs became eligible for the Talkery draw."

"But *you* should also remember, Pop 899," said the Pantek, "that the long struggle was ended by the threat of the wuglings to refuse drunifikation."

"You do not think that too frequent a change of fashun might involve too much labour for the cloth-wugs?" Pop 899 asked.

"Naturally the changes would not have to be too frequent," the Pantek said. "How often does the fashun change in Boojumania?" he turned to ask me.

"Roughly, I should say every year," I replied. "But you will bear in mind, Nob 9, that the average lifetime of a Boojum wug is still not yet half the age at which a

Lunatic wug leaves Lunamania. Might I with the greatest diffidence suggest that a change of fashun every three years should satisfy any Lunatic wug?"

"Pop 899 made a good point when he queried the economic wisdom of changing the fashun too frequently," said the President. "My own opinion is that a change every ten years should satisfy the most fidgety wug. At the same time, I think we should regard any Action that Talkery may pass as experimental. Once we have accepted the principle that wugs will no longer wear forks and allow them to wear spoons we may find that this feeling of fashun will be too strong for us to oppose. On second thoughts I take back my ten-year change and substitute five years, with the promise that if so frequent a change is found to upset the economy of the Republic, Talkery will insist on a longer period between the changes."

The Manager of Drunery asked the Pantek if it was known whether the spoons worn by the wuglings or the forks worn by the wugs was the older dress.

"That we do not know," the Pantek replied. "But it can be taken as certain that in Lunatia at any rate the forks worn by the wugs of to-day were already being worn before the Abominable War."

The President shook a reproachful finger at me.

"See what you've done with your revolutionary Boojum notions, Bosworth One."

"I assure you, Dad 333, that I did not indulge in any kind of propaganda."

At this the President, the Pantek and the Manager of Drunery rocked backwards and forwards in their chairs, laughing loudly.

"He has not been indulging in propaganda!" the President gasped, "and then went off into another fit of uproarious mirth.

"What *are* they laughing at?" I whispered to Tin Pan.

"I do not know, Mr Bosworth. Propaganda is a very serious offence in the Celestial Chinese Republic," he murmured back.

"Unless it is propaganda for Communism, I suppose."

"That is not propaganda. That is truth, Mr Bosworth."

While Tin Pan and I were whispering to one another, the three Lunatics recovered their composure, but when I asked them what I had said to make them laugh like that they started to laugh again. At last the Pantek recovered his gravity.

"You must excuse our unlunatised behaviour, Bosworth One," he said. "But you have used a Lunatic word which must mean something different in Boojum talk. For us, propaganda is the instrument of drunifikation.

"I shall show you one to-morrow, when Dad 333 wishes me to take you round the Seminary and let you see something of our drunes," said Pop 899. "If you will come to the Drunery Office at D-time I shall be attending for you. The Drunery Office is next to the Lookalty, where you have already visited. The Seminary is forty oops from Pinkhall, ten oops beyond Lunatic Ninth Town."

"Tod 51 is too young to visit the Seminary," said the President, "but he can take you to the Office of Drunery where Pop 899 will take charge of you. And I must add a word of warning. It is strictly against the rules of the Everlasting Lunatic Republic for a wug to be told anything about the Seminary. I do not suppose that my mother would encourage you to talk, but wugs are more curious than mugs, and even my mother might be tempted to ask questions," said the President.

"I do not think Sex 715 would do that," the Pantek put in.

"Nor do I, Nob 9, but it is right that Bosworth One and Tin Pan One should know our rules."

"May I be permitted to make an observation, Comrade Dad?" Tin Pan asked. Even now, after nearly a year's residence in the Lunatic Republic, Tin Pan has been unable to drop the prefix 'Comrade'. He *will* put it in, and then thinking it does not suit a number leaves out the number.

"Any observation you wish to make, Tin Pan One," the President told him.

"Far be it from me to presume to take part in any discussion about women's clothes . . . about the dress of wugs . . . but it is my duty to make clear that Mr Bosworth . . . that Bosworth One was speaking for a comparatively small and a comparatively unimportant part of Boojumania when he gave his account of fashion. We in the Prosperity Union of Asia, which thrives under the infallible guidance of the Celestial Chinese Republic, consider fashion to be an example of Western decay. We also regard revisionism as treachery to Marxian ideology, and the proposal for the wugs of the Lunatic Republic to substitute spoons for forks in their attire would be regarded by us as a dangerous example of revisionism."

"You are talking nonsense, Mr Tin Pan," I said sharply; as the President and his two guests had understood very little of Tin Pan's speech, they seemed inclined to agree with me.

Before we left the Pink House the President took me aside and asked me to keep to myself the decision about the proposal to let the wugs of the Lunatic Republic wear spoons of different lengths.

"The wugs will chatter about it among themselves, but it would seem a want of nuclearity if, prior to the talkation in Talkery that will be required before such a change is made, it was known that I or the Pantek had expressed our opinions. Please ask Tin Pan One to be silent also. Ah, that reminds me. What is revisionism? And what is Marxian ideology?"

"Neither question is easy to answer in a few words, Dad 333, but when I go again to the Omnibum I shall try to answer them to Nob 9, who will know how to translate my Boojum explanation into comprehensible Lunatic."

"You are right," said the President. "We regard Nob 9 as the wisest mug in the Republic, and it makes me glad to know how warmly he approves of the reception we gave you when you first came to Lunamania."

"We shall never forget what we owe to you personally, Dad 333," I assured him with fervour.

"You owe something to my mother, Bosworth One, and you repay her by putting ideas into her head at the age of a hundred and eighty-six," the President chuckled.

"Well, if Nob 9 is the wisest mug in the Lunatic Republic, I am certain that the wisest wug is Sex 715," I told her son. Although the President dismissed with a deprecatory gesture the compliment to his mother, I was aware that it pleased him quite a lot.

"And you do understand, don't you," the President wound up, "that the details of your visit to the Seminary to-morrow are not for the chatterbox in your hive? As you know, we dislike the word privilege intensely. Nevertheless, I have to admit that we do grant certain privileges to hivers when they attain their majority, as we call it, or become a hundred and twenty-one years old. For instance, at that age mugs and wugs become eligible to draw for a seat in Talkery and mugs but never wugs may visit the Seminary."

"You call a hundred and twenty-one a hiver's majority," I commented. "A Boojum attains his majority in my part of Boojumania when he is twenty-one."

"Twenty-one?" the President repeated in amazement. "No wonder you are still so backward in Boojumania compared with us."

"We have such a respect for youth that our mugs are afraid to acquire wisdom in case their fellow-mugs should suppose they were growing old. The result is that when our statesmen obtain office they have become old without wisdom," I declared.

"Beddo, Bosworth One. I must not keep you longer. It will soon be K-time."

I was preparing to give Dad 333 the farewell salute to which the President is entitled, but he anticipated me with a warm clasp of my hand, and a few moments later Tin Pan and I were walking with the self-walk back to Hive 6.

At D-time next day we presented ourselves at the Office of Drunery, where Pop 899 received us in his ritery.

"It will take us some time to reach the Seminary," he said, "and so I think we should start at once. Tuk 205 will accompany us."

I asked who Tuk 205 was.

"He is the Chief Fertiliser and Second Manager of Drunery."

"I suppose he is a medical mug?" I asked.

"Medical?" Pop 899 repeated. "What is medical?"

I tried to explain.

"But we do not have this illness or sickness as you call it in the Lunatic Republic."

"So sanaton must be germ-proof and virus-proof," I said to Tin Pan.

"You have no fevers, no chills, no diseases of any kind, not even any slipped discs?" he asked incredulously.

"Such words are all strange to me," the Manager of Drunery declared.

"But when a wug has her mugling or wugling, is there nobody to help her?" I asked.

"We have helpwugs whose duty it is to attend the new arrival in Lunamania for three months and prepare the bixifit for the bluebag."

"For the bluebag?" I exclaimed.

"That is what we call a newly arrived mugling or wugling," said Pop 899.

"But even if you never have illness or sickness in the Lunatic Republic," I persisted, "surely you must sometimes have accidents, for instance among the digmugs in the various mines?"

"If it is a serious accident the mug always leaves Lunamania at once. He is given the devitalot which makes him turn white, the same that is given to the hiver who has finished the hundred and ninety-nine years of his existence in Lunamania."

"You never try a surgical operation?" And I tried to explain what that was.

"But if a digmug lost an arm or a leg he would not want to stay in Lunamania because he would be unusual. One of the chairmugs from the Office of Arrival and Departure would be called to the quickspeak and he would bring the devitalot for the cookwug."

I was just going to ask how the fertilisers obtained their position when Tuk 205 entered the ritery. Later I ascertained that when a Lunatic attains his majority of a hundred and twenty-one years and becomes eligible for fertilisation he is chosen for the post by the luck of the draw.

When Tuk 205 joined us, we left the Office of Drunery and took the upstep to the self-walk.

I reckoned that well over two hours of Earth time had

G

passed before we reached Lunatic Ninth Town, on the outskirts of which we left the self-walk and walked about a hundred yards to a gate guarded by two lookmugs who when they saw the Manager of Drunery approaching stood on their heads. I asked why the lookmugs had not stood on their heads when the First Look of the Lookalty had approached the silon gate of the Roundabout look-house.

"Because that is a silon gate. This is not a silon gate and the lookmugs on look must stand on their heads to show that they are paying attention."

I found the explanation difficult to grasp, but left it at that.

When the lookmugs were back on their feet, one of them opened the gate for us to pass through to an upstep that led to a self-walk on which we were the only passengers.

"Nobody can walk here unless he has a special licence from the Office of Drunery," Pop 899 informed us. "Ten oops from now we shall come to the Seminary Reservation."

"I notice there is no bixifit growth here," I remarked as I looked down at the grey wilderness over which we were passing.

"We could not have bixifit here because the keep-down is always turned off."

Knowing the effect of this, I could readily appreciate that bixifit growth would indeed offer a problem in such conditions.

We must have been moving for nearly half an hour across this waste before we saw ahead of us the silvon fence that runs all the way round the Lunatic Republic; when we were still about a quarter of a mile away from it, the self-walk curved to the right and a few minutes later we descended the downstep, the self-walk continuing in a wide sweep to go back in the same direction as that from which we had come. I hoped we should not find the keepdown turned off when we reached the ground, for I had no desire to bounce on to the magnetised gate in front of us. However, the lookmugs on look at the bottom of the downstep knew their job, and all was well. Nor did they stand on their heads to salute the Manager of Drunery.

When we had passed through the gate, we went into what appeared to be a kind of reception hall, where we were greeted by Rum 702, the Keeper of the Seminary. Half a dozen mugs passed us going in the direction of the gate and carrying boxes. We were told that they were fertilisers on their way to the Office of Arrival and Departure.

Outside the reception hall a self-walk not more than a couple of feet above the ground was moving beside a wide road along which were driving self-wagons loaded with bixifit.

"But soon the bixifit self-walk for the growth on the other side of Ninth Lunatic Town will be constructed, and that will walk directly to the cookeries of the drunehives," Pop 899 told us. "It should have been constructed long ago, but it was necessary first to complete the fence, and that was a slow business because of the difficulty of obtaining the silon from the Great Lunarian Waste. Many digmugs had to leave Lunamania before it was finished and our fertilisers were kept very busy."

I could not help feeling rather pleased to hear that even the Lunatic Republic still had its labour problems.

As we were walking with the self-walk I saw what looked to me like golfers playing their game across a stretch of pink links.

"Those are gimper-drunes," said Pop 899. "They remain for ten years longer in Lunamania than the ordinary drunes and they spend those ten years playing hitball. There is a feeling in Pinkhall that they should leave Lunamania when the other drunes leave, that is when they are forty years old, but I have pushed strongly that they should be allowed to enjoy these ten years and Bum 444, the Manager of Gimpery, has pushed behind me."

"They seem to be playing a game very similar to a game we call golf in Boojumania, the object of which is to knock a little ball into eighteen holes one after another with the fewest strokes."

"Yes, that sounds very like hitball," said Tuk 205, "except that in hitball there are ninety-nine holes for each game and when a hitter has hit his ball into a hole he is allowed to hit his opponent's ball as far away as possible from the next hole. But if he does that he must win the next three holes or start from the beginning again."

"The game must take a long time to finish," I observed.

"Yes, yes, sometimes a game will last for several months," Pop 899 agreed.

Soon after this information about hitball, we began to pass the sanaton hives in which the drunes lived, all of them only six storeys high.

"There are ninety-nine hives, each with a hundred and one drunes or drunelings," Pop 899 continued. "We will take the next downstep and see one of the hives."

"Won't the drunes object to strangers like Tin Pan One and myself staring at them?"

"No, no," Tuk 205 put in. "The novelty will please them, and it is good for them to be pleased."

Nevertheless, I felt embarrassed when we entered the sittery of one of the hives and saw about twenty listless mugs in blue nightgowns lolling about in what looked like magenta-coloured deck-chairs.

"I notice that they all have moustaches and beards."

Pop 899 did not understand what I had said.

"Hair on their faces," I went on.

"Ah, yes, all drunes have lipmould and jawmould."

"Do they sit about like this all day?"

"No, no, these drunes will soon be in the cookery preparing Second Eat."

"Oh, they have to do their own cooking?"

"We could not allow cookwugs to prepare the bixifit for them. No wug in the Lunatic Republic has ever seen a drune. Have you the word 'love' in Boojumania?" Pop 899 asked.

"We certainly have."

"Is it a terrible word for you as it is for us?"

"On the contrary, we are very fond of it."

"I asked that because you did not bloosh when I said it."

"Nor did you," I pointed out to Pop 899.

"That is because I have been Manager of Drunery for fifteen years. I have three more years still, unless my name is drawn again. If it is, I shall have another nine years. All mugs past a hundred and twenty-one who have a nine in their number are drawn for the Management of Drunery, and I have been drawn twice."

"So you are a hundred and thirty-six years old," I said.

"Very good. You number well, Bosworth One."

"But don't drunes have any kind of recreation?" I asked. "I should have thought they would need it."

"They have the see-all, and they can chatter to one another."

"But what have they got to chatter about?"

"They can chatter about what they have seen on the see-all."

I was glad when we left those listless drunes in their

blue nightgowns. I found the sight of them depressing.

The druneling hives were much more cheerful. Indeed, I could have fancied from the jolly shouts of these drunelings at play that I was watching human children. As it was not considered necessary to teach them anything about anything until they were ready to be given what we call sex instruction, they were as free as the noble little savages of a mythical golden age. Whatever the disadvantages of their adult life, they did at least have these first years of happiness. In that they were more fortunate than the muglings and wuglings who were sent to school at two and who for eighteen years had to learn technology, at the end of which time (unless they were lucky enough to draw a ten-plus ticket in the draw and so continue at school for another ten years to become knowalls and chairmugs) they had to spend many years as digmugs or workmugs in which very little of the technology they had learnt was any use to them. Although it is true that everybody in the Lunatic Republic has an equal share of its products, I cannot help feeling that the Lunatic way of life is a warning to the way of life of which we are now in pursuit on earth. During that talk I had with the Pantek I felt that he wondered whether in gaining so much the Lunatic Republic had not lost more.

After we had seen the drunelings at play, we visited some of the laboratories, where the large staff of fertilisers were preparing the vitalots necessary to sustain the drunes in their efforts to preserve the population of the Everlasting Lunatic Republic. We saw the instrument called a propaganda, my use of which term in an earthly sense had caused such merriment at J-time in the Pink House.

I must confess that I left the Seminary Reservation with profound relief. I found it painful to reflect that the great-great-grandfather of the President or the Pantek was one of those listless creatures in a blue nightgown with lipmould and jawmould on their faces.

"I am not surprised," I said to the Manager of Drunery, "that you do not allow anybody under the age of a hundred and twenty-one to see the Seminary. And you were certainly right to make it absolutely forbidden to wugs of any age."

"Well, as Chief Fertiliser I ought not to say this, Bosworth One," said Tuk 205, "but I hope our knowalls will succeed at last in making life out of not-life."

"Yes, yes, I can easily imagine a time in the future of the Everlasting Lunatic Republic," Pop 899 added, "when drune will be as terrible a word as love is to-day."

I know that my account of the Seminary has left much unsaid, but I found our visit such a depressing experience that I have been glad to avoid possible censorship by saying nothing about much that we were shown. I wish that our earthly advocates of artificial insemination could see those listless Lunatic drunes in their blue nightgowns lolling about in those magenta deck-chairs.

## Chapter 12

THE House of Talkery, like the Pink House and the Kurarium, is built of karnikon and would form a complete globe if the bottom of it had not been as it were sliced off to provide accommodation for the members when they are in session, as they always are during D-time, day in day out. On one side are three rows of carmine benches for the mug members and on the other side three rows of carmine benches for the wug members.

Before wugs were granted the right to sit in Talkery, the two parties in the House consisted of Blues and Pinks, and I am informed that the proceedings largely consisted of awkward questions being asked by the Blues about the way the Pinks as officials were carrying out their duties. I am also informed that the opposition of the Pinks to letting wugs sit in Talkery was finally overcome by an Action making Pinks in the Management Offices ineligible for Talkery and restricting the Pink membership to the chairmugs and knowalls who were no longer actively engaged on official work. These were known as Purps, although they continued to wear pink attire. Later, when wugs became members of Talkery, Pinks and Purps were both excluded from it, at the same time, any recommendation sent by Pinks had to be talkated and the Pinks supporting such recommendations took part in the talkation. It may be remembered that when we arrived in the Lunatic Republic the President himself made a recommendation to Talkery which was immediately accepted and an Action authorising our entertainment as welcome guests of the Republic was quickly passed.

It was further enacted when wugs became eligible for Talkery, that in future all M.T.s, mugs and wugs alike, should *ipso facto* become Pinks. Apparently there had been a tendency just because they were Blues for the Blues to oppose Pink recommendations, and it was felt that if they became Pinks themselves this tendency would disappear, as indeed it did.

It was the Talkeroon himself, Jaz 119, who provided me with all this information, and both Tin Pan and I were invited to attend talkations whenever we felt like doing so, being given the freedom of the Talkeroon's own peepery, which was reached by an upstep on the right of the entrance. Tin Pan became so absorbed with his researches in the Omnibum that he seldom attended talkations, but I who was more interested in the present of the Lunatic Republic than its remote past, attended frequently. Moreover, Tin Pan's scientific training took him around all the Lunatic factories, and there is nothing I dislike more than being taken round factories, unable as I am to grasp what is going on.

To come back to the House of Talkery. The ninety-nine mugs on one side and the ninety-nine wugs on the other side had to address any remarks they wished to make to the Stool, and preface what they had to say with 'Respectable Talkeroon'. The Speaker's Chair in our own House of Commons is the equivalent of the Talkeroon's Stool in the House of Talkery, and it is in fact a three-legged stool raised above the level of the members' benches by a dais, the stool and the dais both being made of a glassy substance the colour of port-wine.

And now I come to the most remarkable feature of the House of Talkery. Except for the karnikon floor, the carmine benches, the Talkeroon's Stool, and a gallery above the entrance in which are the peeperies of the President, the Pantek and the Talkeroon, the whole of

G*

the rest of the globular walls and ceiling gives a realistic representation of the Great Lunarian Waste, the effect of which is awe-inspiring, and I do not use the expression lightly. The object of this architectural feat, which as far as I can make out was accomplished some five centuries ago, was to offer a perpetual reminder to the M.T.s on their carmine benches at least three hundred feet below the summit of that gigantic globe from what dreadful havoc once upon a time the Lunatic Republic had managed to survive. No description I am able to write can convey the effect of those craters, into the dark depths of which the Members of Talkery gaze whenever they raise their eyes. I have forgotten to mention the word written in great capital letters of some silvery substance on the wall behind the Talkeroon's Stool. This is ALFRAL, which is the Lunatic way of writing ALL FOR ALL.

It was about six months after that party the President's mother gave in the Pink House that I was invited by him to attend the last great talkation that would decide whether wugs should give up wearing forks and adopt the spoon. The President himself was absent, but his mother was there.

"It is good that you should be in Talkery this D-time," Sex 715 said to me as we sat side by side looking down through circular apertures in the peepery at the carmine benches of the ninety-nine wug M.T.s to our left and of the ninety-nine mug M.T.s to our right below. "Yes, you and I, Bosworth One, can feel puffish to think that it was we who started this talkation."

I asked how she thought the voting would go.

"I think we shall win. Pig 22, who is the first pusher for those who wish to abolish forks, is a highly lunatised and brainish wug. She is the mother of the Chief Bigmouth at the Office of Announcement, and Lux 540 will be very puffish to-morrow if he is able to speak a nine-bell announcement that in future wugs will not throw away their spoons after drunifikation."

"When the President and the Pantek were discussing your proposal after they first heard of it, they both seemed doubtful whether the fashion ought to change every year. Indeed, the President thought that if it changed every ten years it would be enough," I told Sex 715.

"My son is a mug, and mugs can be very stupid when they are trying to manage wugs. I am now a hundred and eighty-six, and if the fashun is not to change for ten years I shall have only one change before I leave Lunamania. But be quiet now. The Talkeroon is just going to blow his woo-hoo for the talkation to begin."

When he had sounded his woo-hoo, which resembled the whistle of a football referee, the Talkeroon said something to one of the two Clurks of Talkery who stood on each side of the Stool. This Clurk then walked along the front bench of the wugs and tapped one of them on the head with a small silvery hammer.

"He has tapped Pig 22 with the hammer of eloquence," said the President's mother," bouncing up and down on her seat. "This is going to be exciting."

Many things had surprised me since I arrived in the Lunatic Republic, but the vitality of this wug of a hundred and eighty-six was as surprising as any.

Pig 22 rose to her feet.

"Respectable Talkeroon," she began, "I rise this D-time to propose one of the most important Actions that Talkery has been asked to pass in the whole history of the Everlasting Lunatic Republic." There were approving murmurs of 'listen, listen' from the wug benches. "For more than three thousand years our beautiful young wuglings have been compelled . . ." cries of 'no compulsion' came from the mug benches, and the Talkeroon blew his woo-hoo.

"The venerable members on the mug benches must allow the venerable member who is speaking to speak without interruptions," the Talkeroon said sternly. One of the mug members rose, but before he could say a word the Talkeroon blew his woo-hoo again.

"The venerable member from Eighth Lunatic Town will re-seat himself."

The member at once sat down, and Pig 22 resumed her interrupted speech.

"Respectable Talkcroon, I was about to say that for more than three thousand years our beautiful wuglings on becoming wugs have been compelled to abandon the spoons they wear, and have always worn with such pleasure, in order to put on the forks of which, respectable Talkeroon, I say with intense emfatifikation the wugs of the Everlasting Lunatic Republic are now weary." There was a chorus of 'listen, listen' from the wug benches. "Why are we wugs weary of forks? Because, respectable Talkeroon, forks have remained exactly the same shape since they were first worn. It is true that a hundred years ago there was a prolonged struggle for our wugs to win the right to have footboxes that were not attached to our forks like the footboxes of the muggish leggings. It is true that when we won the right to have these footboxes we decided to put high stumps on them so that we who had been two nails shorter than mugs were now on a level with them. It is true that we wugs of the Everlasting Lunatic Republic then at last became eligible to sit in Talkery. And has not our membership made Talkery more truly representative of the Everlasting Lunatic Republic? (Cries of 'yes, yes' from the wug benches.) I am glad that the venerable members on the benches opposite do not venture to contradict the claim I have just made, and it gives me much pleasure to offer a warm tribute to their nuclearity.

"Respectable Talkeroon, I have said that we are weary of forks, and if I am asked by my venerable friends on the benches opposite whether the abolition of forks for wugs may not lead presently to our becoming weary of spoons I shall reply to that question with a confident negative because it is our intention to prevent any such weariness by changing the length of the spoon every year, the annual length to be settled by a committee of fashunwugs nominated by the Manager of Kulture so that no undue strain shall be put upon the bixifit growth. Respectable Talkeroon, I ask for the assent of Talkery to this lunatised and look-ahead proposal."

The speaker resumed her seat amid loud cheers from the wug benches. One of the Clurks of Talkery now proceeded to tap a mug member on the head with that hammer of eloquence.

"The Clurk has tapped Tax 200," the President's mother commented. "He is against our spoons."

"He has an ill-omened name for Boojum ears," I told her, but before I could explain why, Tax 200 was on his feet.

"Respectable Talkeroon, the venerable lug from Third Lunatic Town . . ." I must interrupt Tax 200 for a moment to explain that in Talkery there is almost as exaggerated an appearance of politeness as there is in our own House of Commons. 'Lug' is a formally respectful way for a mug member to refer to a wug member, and she in turn will always refer to him as a 'jug'. "The venerable lug from Third Lunatic Town who has just addressed the . . . the . . ." Tax 200 hesitated for a moment . . . "the one million twenty-two thousand three hundred and fifty-first Session of the House of Talkery . . ."

The Talkeroon blew his woo-hoo.

"The venerable member from Sixth Lunatic Town is in error. This is the one million twenty-two thousand three hundred and fifty-second Session of the House of Talkery," he declared solemnly.

There was an indignant murmur from the wug benches and from those members on the mug benches who were not in agreement with the speaker.

"That was a stupid blumber for Tax 200 to make," the President's mother commented with obvious satisfaction. A blumber is a mistaken number, and a Lunatic who commits one is held guilty of unlunatised behaviour; numbers are very important in the Lunatic Republic."

"Respectable Talkeroon, I offer my humble exkusifikation to you and to this House for saying the one million twenty-two thousand three hundred and fifty-first Session when I should have said the one million twenty-two thousand three hundred and fifty-second Session."

"The exkusifikation of the venerable member from Sixth Lunatic Town is accepted by the Stool," said the Talkeroon.

"I have listened with apprehension, to the arguments of the venerable lug on the benches opposite," Tax 200 resumed, "for I ask myself whether the intention behind what may seem to some of you a purely wuggish concern is to raise at a future date a much graver issue. I shall remind the House that, when the wugs of the Everlasting Lunatic Republic were successful in detaching their footboxes from their forks and adding to them high stumps, those extra nails put them on an apparent level with mugs."

At this there were cries of 'real not apparent!' from the wug benches.

"Those high stumps," the speaker continued, "were a prelude to the membership of Talkery that venerable lugs opposite now enjoy. I ask whether this superficially trivial change in the dress of wugs from forks to spoons may not be the prelude to a demand to take part in the draw for Managerial Office which under the constitution of the Everlasting Lunatic Republic is open only to mugs."

Pig 22 rose immediately.

"Respectable Talkeroon, on a point of order, is the venerable jug opposite entitled to imply that the Action of Talkery which admitted the wugs of the Everlasting Lunatic Republic to sit in this House was obtained by a trikifikation?"

This question set off such an indignant babble on the wug benches that the Talkeroon had to blow his woohoo for silence.

"The venerable member from Sixth Lunatic Town is not entitled to attribute to the venerable member from Third Lunatic Town any ulterior motives. The Action before the House is 'That this House accepts the proposal that in future the wugs of the Everlasting Lunatic Republic shall wear spoons instead of forks with the proviso that the cloth of the old forks shall be used for the new spoons.' I must ask the venerable member from Sixth Lunatic Town to confine his talking strictly to the Action."

"Respectable Talkeroon, I bow to your rulifikation," said Tax 200, "and I hasten to add that my opposition to this action does not depend at all on the answer to the question I asked just now. What utterly perturb me are the economic consequences of this abrupt and ill-considered departure from the immemorial dress of our

Lunatic wugs. We mugs hold our wugs in the highest esteem, and indeed how else could we hold them, for without them we should never have arrived in Lunamania? But that esteem must not blind us to the possible economic consequences for our Republic if we put too heavy a strain on our supplies of cloth. I applaud the proviso in the Action which insists that new spoons are to be fitted from the cloth of the old forks should they be abolished. But I must draw attention to one remark made by the venerable lug who pushed this Action. She said, and I wobbled upon my feet as I listened to her, respectable Talkeroon, she said it was the intention of the wugs to change the length of their spoons annually (murmurs on the mug benches). I do not wonder that some of my venerable friends on this side of the House are as much perturbed as I am. It is all very well for the venerable lug opposite to say that this change of length will be settled by a committee of fashunwugs nominated by the Manager of Kulture, but it is not fair to burden the Manager responsible for the maintenance of the bixifit growth with such a task. I venture to assert that the bixi we eat is a more important part of the growth than the fit we wear. Can we be assured that the additional supplies of the fit will not imperil the production of the bixi? Suppose, lugs and jugs, that this committee should decide in some future year that spoons are to reach to the ankles. Imagine the extra demand upon the bixifit. It will be a sorry day for the Republic when its hivers are denied their full plates of bixifit because our wugs have put the length of their spoons before the bodily needs of our hivers. We shall be told by those who support this Action that we can rely on the Management of Kulture to guard against such a disaster. I have the fullest confidence in the Management of Kulture, but I do not consider it is right to upset their present estimates for the annual supply of cloth by making them dependent on the whims of a committee of fashunwugs. Surely we have been perfectly content with the forks which the venerable lugs on the benches opposite are now wearing this D-time, and have always been wearing from the year when our mothers of long long ago first designed them? This Action, if passed, will disturb the everlasting sameness of our Lunatic way of life. I beg to push it back for rejection."

The Talkeroon now rose to say that the Knowful Pantek was ready to address the House if the House desired to hear his words. There was loud applause on both sides. This was followed by a threefold knock on the great doors leading into Talkery. The two Clurks went down and tapped three times on the inner side of the doors with their little hammers. Then they opened the doors to admit the Pantek. He was wearing round his neck a chain of some bright metal similar to that which the President put on when he went to obtain from Talkery an Action to allow Tin Pan and myself to be the guests of the Lunatic Republic. He advanced between the two rows of benches to the Stool, and mounting the dais stood beside the Talkeroon and began to speak:

"Respectable Talkeroon and Venerable Members of Talkery, I have to inform you that a thorough enquiry has now been made into the effects of abolishing the forks which the wugs of the Everlasting Lunatic Republic now wear after the age of drunifikation is over, whether they have or have not drawn mother tickets, and of substituting spoons for such forks. Twenty-four knowalls under my chairmugship have explored every self-walk to reach a decision about the merits of this push and have finally agreed unanimously to recommend it as an Action which Talkery may pass with benefit to the nuclearity of the Everlasting Lunatic Republic. We have had the advantage during our anxious enquiry of consultation with the highly regarded Manager of Kulture, Vej 561, and as the result of such precious consultation we wish to recommend to Talkery that if and when it may decide to pass an Action authorising the substitution of spoons for the forks now worn it should state clearly in such an authorisation that spoons must remain the same length for a period of not less than five years. We are of the opinion that an annual change of length might entail serious economic difficulties."

"How like a mug," the President's mother commented. "He does not understand that twice as much cloth is used in making a fork as a spoon."

"But the House can hardly vote against the Action after what the Pantek has said," I pointed out. "And, you know, at first, the President was in favour of allowing the change of length only every ten years."

"Yes, yes, all mugs are the same," Sex 715 sighed.

After the Pantek had delivered his recommendation, the talkation was resumed, but it was fairly soon evident that the opponents of the change were in a small minority; and when the Talkeroon called upon the House to divide not more than a dozen members, and they all mugs, stood on their feet. The other members were all standing on their heads. I should explain that when an Action has been talkated those members in favour of it stand on their heads, those against it on their feet.

"Won't it be rather awkward for wugs to stand on their heads when they are wearing long spoons?" I asked Sex 715.

"As easy as eating bixifit," she said with a grin.

"But wouldn't it be even easier if those in favour held up their right hands and those against held up their left hands?"

"In the Lunatic Republic both hands are equal."

"They are both equal in Boojumania, but we distinguish one from the other."

"Then they are not equal," the President's mother declared firmly. "Distinction is inequality."

"Sex 715," I argued, "mugs and wugs are equal in the Lunatic Republic, but there is a distinction between them."

"No, there is a difference between the muggish body and the wuggish body, but there is no distinction between them since our wugs have been wearing footboxes with high stumps."

"Then won't wearing spoons instead of forks create this very distinction you condemn?"

She pondered for a moment before she answered my question.

"No, I do not think so," she replied at last, "but all the same I am glad that none of the opposition mugs raised that point. We were clever in putting up a Lunatic Town wug like Pig 22 to push our case. There is always, you know, a slight inclination among the Town hivers to suppose that the City hivers are being puffish."

"I'm afraid you are a little disappointed that the fashion is going to change every five years instead of annually."

"Yes, it means that I shall only see two changes of fashun before I leave Lunamania; but half a vitalot is better than no vy, and perhaps the chairmugs in the Kulture Office will find that the demand upon the bixifit growths is not so heavy as they fear."

The next day I took what I have written about Lunamania to the Pantek and asked him to read it and make any corrections or excisions he considered desirable.

"You must read it to me, Bosworth One," he said. "I

am not able to manage your ancient complicated spelling and the strange wriggles of your letters."

I told Nob 9 that I had considered using the simplified Lunatic spelling, but that as I hoped my brief account of the Lunatic Republic would be read some day in the future by Boojums, I did not want them to have to wait until they had mastered simplified spelling before they could read what I had written. We were still arguing about a simplified alphabet ('lettery' is the Lunatic word) invented by a Boojum knowall called Shaw who left Boojumania nearly fifty years ago.

So for the next few days I went regularly at D-time to the Omnibum and in the Pantek's ritery I read aloud to him this account.

"You will understand, Nob 9, that I have merely tried to give the general sense of the various chatters I have had since I arrived here. I kept notes in a notebook, but that notebook is now full. My attempt to record the talkation about spoons and forks used up the last empty pages."

"No, I certainly cannot hear myself speaking as you have made me speak," the Pantek said with a smile as he turned over the pages describing the first visit to the Omnibum of Tin Pan and myself.

"If you will let me read to you that chatter we had, it will not sound so stilted."

"Stilted?" he repeated.

I tried to explain to him our use of the word and its derivation.

"You have given me an idea," he said. "About sixty years ago, digmugs searching for blankon on the edge of the Great Lunarian Waste found six implements which resemble these stilts you speak of. They are now in the Kurarium. We have never been able to imagine what purpose they served; perhaps they were used when there were still the remains of what you call water on Lunamania and which the earliest chronicles refer to as joose."

"We have the same word for the moisture in fruit, but we spell it j-u-i-c-e."

The Pantek shook his head with a smile at such Boojumatic spelling.

"And what is fruit?" he asked. "I suppose you spell that f-r-u-i-t?"

"We do."

My answer made him laugh.

When I had finished reading my manuscript to the Pantek he told me that it was difficult for him to judge it because so much of it was taken up in describing such ordinary matters that they hardly seemed worth the trouble of recording.

"I will make you a promise, Nob 9. When I have had more practice with your simplified spelling and have mastered the Lunatic vocabulary more thoroughly I will write an account of Boojumania, and when I do that you will find absolutely extraordinary what I consider so ordinary as hardly to be worth recording."

The Pantek nodded his recognition of that before he went on with his comments on my manuscript.

"Yes, I am bearing in mind that your account is written for Boojums, not for Lunatics. It is occasionally a little confused, but that is not surprising, because you were trying to give your first impressions and your mind was overcrowded with novelties. I rather wish you had amplified the account of this fizzer in which you came to us. But no doubt if you write for us an account of Boojumania we shall be better able to understand the strange and extremely unlunatised behaviour of these creatures you call Chinese. Tin Pan One has made a favourable impression on us at the Omnibum, and I find it hard to understand how he can be of the same species as these Chinese who put you in what you call a prison. That word does not exist in Lunatic, and I trust it never will. What are bananas? You speak of what seems to be a kind of vitalot you were given in the fizzer and you say it tasted of bananas."

I told the Pantek that the banana was now almost the equivalent of bixifit in Boojumania, except that our technologists had not yet discovered a way of turning its skin into cloth.

"But bixifit tastes of nothing," said the Pantek.

"That is true, Nob 9, but to our Boojum palates all eats in the Lunatic Republic taste of nothing, except that crimson vitalot I tasted at Second Eat with the gimpers, and your delicious Vitalot 12."

"Yes, that does indeed taste of something," the Pantek agreed, "and I look forward to hearing more about the various Boojum eats which you say it reminded you of. There is one point you prudently do not make clear. You do not explain how a wugling becomes the mother of a drune."

"I am not sure myself."

"It is a closely guarded secret, and I am glad you did not attempt an explanation, because if you had I should have asked you to suppress it."

And then the Pantek told me how it was that no wug ever knew that she had become the mother of a drune. However, I am not at liberty to reveal this secret, and so my unimaginable readers of the future will have to be kept guessing.

"I think it will be better if your scratch (that is Lunatic for a manuscript) remains in the bookery of the Omnibum," the Pantek decided. "There only by per- mission of the Pantek himself will it be made available to a knowall who wishes to know the facts of your com-

ing to Lunamania. The Kurarium has your Boojum
dress, but if your scratch is displayed in the Kurarium
the Karetaker will want you to make chatter about it on
the tell-speak. That might involve removing from your
scratch some of the remarks about our way of life in the
Lunatic Republic. But if your scratch will only be read
by duly accredited knowalls, we need not be so fussish.''

The very next day I added the substance of this inter-
view with the Pantek to my manuscript and I shall hand
it over to him on the anniversary of the day when Tin
Pan and I landed on the Moon.

The Lunatic year is a day less than ours, consisting of
thirteen booths of twenty-eight days each. What we call
a month is called a booth in Lunatic. The progress of the
calendar is announced every week by a bigmouth from
the Office of Announcement. The tell-bell rings and
everywhere hear-alls announce: 'Now begins the second
week of the third booth in the three thousand and forty-
eighth year of the Everlasting Lunatic Republic' or
whatever date falls to be announced. The first day of the
week is called Wunday followed by Tooday, Threeday,
Forday, Fiday, Sixiday and Senday.

As I write that gen about the calendar, I realise how
much has been omitted from this account that a good
technologist would have known how to describe. I con-
sole myself with the reflection that if any Boojums—
already after a year I think of my fellow-creatures on the
Earth as Boojums—if any of them, I say, do reach the
Lunatic Republic and read what I have written, they
will certainly be technologically much better equipped
in the dawn of the Automatic Age to appreciate the
achievements of the Lunatic knowalls than I have been.
My hope is that I have been able to record, however
inadequately, the gratitude I feel to the many Lunatics
who have treated the two visitors from another world

with such consistent kindliness and such extreme generosity. My still unimaginable readers who have read this brief account of the Lunatic Republic will have understood by now that to a Lunatic to be unusual is to offend against all the ideals of lunatisation. There is no precept in the Lunatic code of morality more solemnly esteemed than 'Sameness is strength'. Above the entrance to every hive you may read the word SIS in letters of glittering carmine. To be unusual is a stigma; to be deliberately 'unsissy' would be unthinkable. Indeed, the epithet is reserved for those Lunarians of three millenniums ago whose unsissy way of life destroyed themselves and nearly destroyed all Lunamania.

Money does not exist in the Lunatic Republic even as a word. Yet it must have existed in Lunaria, as far as I can gather from the earliest Lunatic chronicles; otherwise the tribute imposed on Lunatian pilgrims who came to worship A, the Mother of Life invisible to them, is inexplicable. I once tried to explain to a small gathering of knowalls our monetary system on Earth. They laughed at the notion of money being used as a token, but when I went on to speak of interest from invested money their laughter stopped and they sat in horrified amazement as if they were listening to a tale of unnatural vice.

I need hardly add that taxation is unknown in the Lunatic Republic, where every mug and wug performs the service allotted to him or her by the luck of the draw. That also eliminates politics and the politician. When I tried to explain our politics and politicians I felt as if I were talking about a loathsome disease spread by noxious parasites, such was the obvious disgust of my listeners. I was not much more successful with trades unions, the need for them being incomprehensible;

when I told them about strikes, the expression of disgust returned.

And now as I lay down my scratcher (spelt skratzer), as a pen is called here, and turn over the thick pages of riton on which I have scratched my feeble attempts to communicate an experience which is as incommunicable as if I were writing in a dream, I am suddenly seized with an immense nostalgia for our imperfect earth. Ruthless ambition, jealousy, pride, yes, even greed and envy seem less undesirable, and love how much more desirable in this mechanically perfect Lunatic Republic on the other side of the Moon.

When I had come to the end of my account I took it up to the Pantek's ritery in order to read him my conclusion, and as I was reading the final sentence we were startled by a tremendous crash somewhere beyond Pinkhall. This was followed by what I can only describe as the infuriated buzz from a gigantic hive suddenly overturned.

"What can have happened?" the Pantek exclaimed as he hurried out of his ritery, to return a few minutes later much agitated.

"The worst has happened," he told me gravely. "The utterly worst! A Boojum fizzer has fallen on Hive 6 and several hivers left Lunamania at once. Mercifully it is D-time; otherwise many more might have left." He hurried to the quickspeak. "Tell Tin Pan One the Pantek wishes him to come at once to the Pantek's ritery."

Nob 9 said nothing while he was waiting for Tin Pan; he stood listening to that menacing buzz that seemed to rise from all over Lunatic City.

"It is certainly not a Chinese fizzer," Tin Pan declared as he entered the ritery. "It may be a Russian fizzer, but I think it is more probably an American fizzer."

"Tin Pan One," said the Pantek quickly, "it would be wiser if you did not appear familiar with this fizzer. You and Bosworth One are both in danger of leaving Lunamania. I do not myself believe that either of you have had anything to do with this fizzer, but when something like this happens, nuclearity can vanish in a moment, and it is most unfortunate that the hive on which this Boojum fizzer fell was the hive where you have your eatings and beddings."

"But how could any mug or wug in the Lunatic Republic suppose Tin Pan and I were responsible for this fizzer?" I exclaimed. Yet I must admit that I felt a good deal less sure of the answer than I tried to sound.

"You may trust me to do all I can to make that evident," said the Pantek. "I hope I shall be successful."

"After all," I argued, "Boojum fizzers and round-abouts have been falling on Lunamania for nearly forty years. There was that roundabout with the monkey which fell not far from the silon fence surrounding the Republic, and that was some years before Tin Pan One and I came to Lunamania."

"Yes, yes," the Pantek asserted, "when this unfortunate event is examined with nuclearity it is evident enough that there is no join up with you and Tin Pan One, but as I told you, under the effect of the unusual nuclearity can vanish."

"That is sadly true of Boojumania, Nob 9, but surely lunatised Lunatics will not allow themselves to behave like Boojums?" I almost pleaded.

The Pantek shook his head.

"I cannot feel too confident. You will both stay here for now. I shall go at once to see the President and I hope to persuade him to let you remain in the Pink House under his protection until nuclearity returns."

When the Pantek left us in his ritery while he was

consulting with the President about the crisis, Tin Pan began to denounce all Americans for the trouble they were causing on the Moon.

"As if they had not caused enough trouble on the Earth," he said bitterly.

"But, Mr Tin Pan, this rocket is just as likely to be a Chinese rocket. Indeed, for all we know it may be a British rocket."

Tin Pan smiled with Celestial condescension. "That I certainly do not believe," he declared.

"I don't know why you should suddenly suppose that the Americans have a better rocket than Heavenly Dragon."

"I do not suppose that, Mr Bosworth."

"After all, if Heavenly Dragon had gone a very little further, you and I might have crashed on Hive 6 and we should both have left Lunamania within a moment of our arrival."

About half an hour later the Pantek came back to the Omnibum to say that the President had agreed to let us stay in the Pink House until Talkery had met to decide about our future.

"But you cannot proceed to the Pink House with safety until the hivers are more quiet," the Pantek warned us. "Now they are going everywhere on the self-walks saying that the Boojums must leave Lunamania at once. Even the digmugs are all hurrying away from the bixifit growths into Lunatic City. I have never seen in my hundred and ninety-one years of life digmugs leaving the growths in the middle of D-time. It is terrible for me. All my eloquence of over thirty years may become a nothing if Talkery passes an Action to-morrow to make counterfizzers against Boojumania. We shall have a Second Abominable War which will destroy all that we have achieved with three thousand years of peace."

The Pantek sank down in his chair and rocked himself backwards and forwards in despair. Presently his ritemug came in to say that the Second Look of the Lookalty wished for a short chatter with him.

"Bring him to see me, Yam 678," said the Pantek.

When the ritemug had retired, I suggested that Tin Pan and I should also withdraw.

"No," he said, "It is good that you should speak with Vim 40, who more than any mug in the Republic wishes that we should make counterfizzers. And when you have convinced him that this fizzer which has fallen on Hive 6 has nothing to do with you I shall ask him to send for a chunk of lookmugs from the Lookalty to escort you to the Pink House."

For a long time the Second Look would say nothing to every argument the Pantek used except reiterate: "Eight hivers in Hive 6 have been forced by this Boojum fizzer to leave Lunamania without a devitalot to turn them white, and if you had not persuaded Talkery to forbid us to build counterfizzers all these years we should be able at this moment to send against Boojumania a hundred counterfizzers with zooms even more potent than those which made the Great Lunarian Waste."

"And what purpose would that serve, Vim 40?" the Pantek asked. "Boojumania would then send fizzers with zooms against the Everlasting Lunatic Republic, and it might well happen that many thousands left Lunamania instead of eight. Remember, Vim 40, that this Boojum fizzer which was zoomless did not know it would fall on a hive."

"That is what you say, Nob 9, but the hivers believe that these two Boojums whom we have treated as lunatised beings were sent here as pokers."

And as the Second Look said this the angry buzzing

of the Lunatics all over the City became loud enough to be called a roar.

"But how could Bosworth One and Tin Pan have poked for Boojumania since they came to Lunatic City?" the Pantek asked impatiently.

"That I do not pretend to know," the Second Look muttered, his mouth set in an obstinate line.

"And you never will know, Vim 40, because if you will consider the question with your usual nuclearity you will understand that they are incapable of communicating with Boojumania."

How thankful I was at this moment that the radio in Heavenly Dragon had conked out! The united efforts of the President and the Pantek would not have been able to keep us in Lunamania if Tin Pan had been fiddling away with switches and buttons during this past year. Then I had an idea.

"Why not build a single counterfizzer and let the Pantek put in it the account of the Lunatic Republic which I have scratched and which he has approved? When the counterfizzer reaches Boojumania, our Boojum knowalls will read my account and take care that in future all fizzers will avoid falling anywhere near the Lunatic Republic?"

"Such a suggestion would have to be placed before Talkery," said the Pantek. "If an Action to build one counterfizzer is talkated, I shall not oppose it. And now, Vim 40, will you send for a chunk of lookmugs to escort Bosworth One and Tin Pan One to the Pink House? The President desires to see them."

To my joy, when the patrol arrived at the Omnibum I found it was under the command of Pup 301.

"Do not be fearful, Bosworth One," he said. "This is a good chunk."

"Tell me, Pup 301. You do not believe that

Tin Pan One and I were responsible for this Boojum fizzer?"

"I do not believe that," he assured me. We shook hands.

It was hardly three hundred yards from the Omnibum to the Pink House, but those three hundred yards on the self-walk were a nightmare. I blessed those stalwart lookmugs led by Pup 301, six in front of us marching with both arms upraised and six more marching backwards behind us until we reached the downstep to the Pink House and were able to walk in comparative quiet along the colonnade to the door.

"Be tranquil," the President told us when we were sitting in his chatterbox. "I am sure that by to-morrow, when Talkery meets, nuclearity will have been restored in Lunatic City."

Tin Pan and I remained in the Pink House all the rest of that day, taking Second Eat and Third Eat with the President and his mother. We shared a room that night, in which the President had had two extra beds put so that we were not cramped when we went to sleep at K-time.

Next day was a Wunday, which I hoped was a good omen for the result of the talkation, and that it would indeed turn out to be a Tin Pan One day and a Bosworth One day. Sex 715 kindly invited us to the bowery when the President with the shining chain round his neck left the Pink House to address Talkery.

"I have no fear," his mother said. "All the wug members know what we wugs owe to Bosworth One for telling us about fashuns in Boojumania. You have not said whether you admired my new spoon, Bosworth One." She smoothed her spoon over her knees. "For the next five years spoons will be ankle-length. We thought it would be wise to begin with long ones, and then perhaps if we change to shorter ones we shall be able to push an Action that will allow us to change every two years, or even every year."

She made me chatter on about the clothes of Boojum wugs until at last the sound of the President's bell was heard coming along the corridor to the Bowery.

"All is well," his mother cried, jumping up and clapping her hands.

"How went it, my son?" she asked when the President came in.

"The Pantek and I have restored nuclearity. Bosworth One and Tin Pan One will not have to leave Lunamania, but whether we shall build a counterfizzer to take Bosworth One's account of the Lunatic Republic to Boojumania has not yet been decided."

In the end Talkery decided against a counterfizzer. All I hope is that a Boojum fizzer does not fall on another hive. Tin Pan and I may not be so lucky next time.